LISETTE DAVENPORT

Whispers of the heart

First edition

ISBN: 978-0-6459323-0-0

This book was professionally typeset on Reedsy.
Find out more at reedsy.com

To my husband for all his support, and to my readers for trusting me.

Chapter One

The clatter of cobblestones rattled the carriage as it rolled through the chaotic streets of London. Though she had been away for five years, the familiar cadence stirred bittersweet memories in Genevieve. Rome's languid pace and sparkling fountains felt a world away from London's hurried crowds and sooty buildings.

Genevieve gazed out the window at the passing townhouses, the brick facades bleeding into a grey blur. People choked the sidewalks, scurrying with brisk efficiency between carriages and carts.

"Nearly home," her mother said, giving her gloved hand a gentle squeeze. Lady Penelope's sapphire necklace glittered like her smile, though Genevieve detected a tightness in her eyes. Even her unflappable mother could not escape the tumult of emotions.

With each turn of the wheels, Genevieve's stomach fluttered. She yearned for the comfort of home yet chafed at the restraints of decorum she had shed in Rome. London's rules of propriety would once again constrict her freedom.

"All of London will be eager to welcome you back," her mother continued, as if sensing Genevieve's qualms.

Genevieve forced a smile, glancing at her younger sister Georgina, who seemed untroubled, gazing out the window with delight. At least one of them relished their return.

The carriage rolled to a stop. Genevieve's heart stumbled, then raced, as the footman opened the door. This was it — her re-entry into London's glittering aristocracy. Its inescapable expectations. She took a deep breath and stepped out.

The familiar cacophony engulfed her—clopping hooves, vendors' cries, the scents of coal smoke and roasting chestnuts. After Rome's sun-filled piazzas, London seemed oppressively dim and chaotic. The looming townhouses blotted out the sky.

Blinking against the onslaught of memories, Genevieve followed her family up the steps of their Mayfair home. The butler greeted them with a bow. "Welcome home, my lord, my ladies."

Genevieve breathed deep into the musty air as she entered the townhouse in what felt like forever. So many memories lingered in these walls. The familiarity of it eased the knot in her stomach, a balm to her frayed nerves. She glanced up at the family portrait on the wall, it had been done before they left, she and Georgina looked so young compared to now; their older brother, Gregory, had been going through a phase of wearing a moustache. Her mother and father looked unchanged.

Her mother glided through the front hall, already issuing orders to the footmen and maids to unpack the carriages. Georgina trailed after her, craning her neck this way and that to take in the soaring ceilings and marble floors.

"Your rooms have been freshly aired and prepared for you, my dears," Lady Penelope said. "I shall leave you to get settled while I check on the kitchens."

Georgina clapped her hands together. "May we explore while the trunks are being brought in?"

"As long as you stay out of the footmen's way. Now, off with you." Their mother shooed them towards the stairs with a smile and wave of her hand.

Georgina grabbed Genevieve's arm, pulling her along in her excitement. "Do you remember how the morning light used to stream through the windows on the third floor? We should see if it's the same."

"In a moment," Genevieve said, stopping at the bottom of the staircase. The familiar scents and sounds tugged at her, but something was not quite right.

An emptiness lingered under it all, as if the life had gone out of the house during their long absence.

She shook off the feeling and followed Georgina up the steps. It would simply take time to grow accustomed to London life once more. Her trepidation would fade, and this house would again feel like the home she remembered.

All it required was patience. A quality she had in abundance.

Genevieve trailed her fingertips along the oak banister as she climbed, the smooth wood worn in places from years of use. At the top of the stairs, she paused again, struck by a wave of nostalgia at the sight of the third-floor corridor.

Georgina turned back, brows knitting together. "What is it?"

"Nothing of consequence." Genevieve waved her on. "Go on ahead. I shall join you momentarily. "Her sister studied her for a long moment before nodding and continuing down the hall.

Alone, Genevieve took a steadying breath and walked to the window at the end of the corridor. Golden sunlight streamed through the panes, dappling the worn floorboards with a warm glow. Just as she remembered. The memory of the real reason they had left to go to Rome surfaced in her mind. The sunlight streaming through the window, his warm breath.

A smile tugged at her lips and the tension eased from her shoulders. No matter the changes in her own life, this house would always remain as the steadfast foundation she could depend upon.

With renewed vigour, she made her way to Georgina's room and found her sister peering out the window onto the street below. "It's wonderful, is it not?" Georgina asked. "Everything is exactly as I recalled."

"Almost everything," Genevieve said, a teasing lilt to her tone. At Georgina's curious glance, she continued, "You seemed to have grown at least a foot taller since we left."

Georgina swatted her arm, unable to hold back a grin. "You are incorrigible."

"And you are far too gullible, dear sister." Genevieve leaned forward to get a better view of the activity below. "How I love teasing you so."

A comfortable silence fell between them as they observed the world beyond, each lost in their own thoughts. London awaited them, familiar yet strange, and together they would face all the challenges and delights it had to offer.

That evening, Genevieve stood before the looking glass in her bedchamber and smoothed the skirts of her azure silk gown. Her reflection stared back at her, pale and wan, a ghostly spectre of the vivacious girl who had left these shores five years prior.

She swallowed against the lump forming in her throat and blinked back the sting of tears. What was wrong with her? She should be ecstatic at the prospect of her first ball since returning home, not battling a maelstrom of anxiety and doubt.

With a sigh, she turned away from the mirror. If she appeared so haggard and worn, how would she ever attract a suitable match? At one and twenty, she was already considered late to enter the marriage mart. Her chances of making a desirable match dwindled with each passing season.

Genevieve sank onto the edge of her bed, clutching the bedpost. The weight of expectations pressed upon her shoulders, relentless and unforgiving. As the eldest daughter, her duty was to her family. She could not fail them. Not when they had sacrificed so much to give her opportunities in Rome.

A rap at the door startled her from her brooding. "Genevieve, the carriage has arrived," her mother said. "Are you ready?"

She swallowed the lump in her throat and summoned a smile. "Yes, Mother. I will be right down."

With a fortifying breath, Genevieve stood. She had a role to play, and she would not disappoint. No matter the cost. Squaring her shoulders, she glided from the room to greet the gilded cage of society that awaited.

* * *

Genevieve gazed out the carriage window as London rolled by in a blur of activity. Crowded streets teemed with people from all levels of society going about their day. The familiar sights and sounds both thrilled and unsettled her.

Part of her longed to throw open the carriage door and lose herself in the maze of byways as she used to do. But she was not a child anymore. She was the eldest daughter of an earl, with responsibilities and expectations to bear.

Genevieve sighed, nerves fluttering in her stomach again. Her first ball since returning to London loomed ahead, and all eyes would be upon her. Judging, assessing, weighing her worth as a prospect. She feared she had forgotten all the intricate steps involved in navigating a ballroom. One misstep could ruin her reputation before the Season had even begun.

A gentle hand covered hers, and Genevieve glanced over to find her mother watching her with understanding eyes. "There is no need to worry yourself into a fret, dearest. You shall do splendidly tonight."

Genevieve attempted a smile, though it came out lopsided. "Everyone will be comparing me to how I was as a girl. I am not the same, Mother. What if I have changed too much?"

"Some things remain constant, like your kind heart and quick wit." Lady Penelope gave her hand a squeeze. "Your beauty and charm will be too captivating for the gentlemen to notice any differences. You are a woman now, Genevieve, and it is time to embrace all the excitement and opportunities that come with it."

Her mother's confidence helped bolster her own. Genevieve's spine straightened, resolution filling her. She would face this new world head-on, just as a St. Claire of Mayfair should. Starting with her first ball, where she was determined to shine.

* * *

The ballroom glittered with candlelight and jewels, a kaleidoscope of colour and sound. Genevieve hovered near the perimeter, clutching a glass of lemonade like a lifeline. Though the familiar strains of a quadrille and polite laughter should have eased her nerves, apprehension coiled in the pit of her stomach.

Each gaze that lingered upon her seemed weighted with judgment. Were her gloves spotless enough? Her countenance pleasant? Her movements graceful? One misstep could ruin her chances and reflect poorly on her family. The crushing weight of expectations threatened to suffocate her. Looking across the room, her eyes met an old friend's. Lord Mordesley. Her breath hitched, her pulse quickened. She had hoped her time in Rome had cured her of her feelings for him, but it seemed she was wrong. She broke their connection, suddenly feeling very warm. She moved from one acquaintance to the next, highly aware her mother would be watching. She danced with one of her brother's old school friends, Lord Daniels, more to keep her mother happy than a desire to dance. Daniels had always had a way to make her laugh, however, his familiarity often stepped too close to impropriety.

With a murmured excuse, Genevieve slipped from the ballroom. The balcony provided a reprieve from prying eyes, a chance to still her trembling hands and gather her wits. A cool breeze washed over her, carrying the scent of hyacinths from the garden below.

In the shadows, she leaned against the balustrade and closed her eyes. How she longed for the sun-drenched piazzas of Rome, for the freedom of anonymity. No expectations, but those she set for herself.

A door creaked open behind her. Genevieve stiffened, clutching at the last vestiges of calm.

"There you are," a familiar baritone said. "I was hoping to find you alone."

Her heart stuttered at the sound of that voice, it was at once soothing and unsettling. Summoning her composure, Genevieve turned to face the Marquess of Mordesley.

The Marquess stood in a pool of golden light; his features softened by shadows. Still, she could discern the hint of a smile on his lips and a curious light in his eyes as he gazed upon her.

Genevieve smoothed her expression into one of polite interest. "My lord. To what do I owe the pleasure?"

"You seemed distressed. I wanted to ensure you were well."

"How very kind." She kept her tone light, belying the tumult within. "'Tis nothing, merely the heat of the ballroom. I required a breath of fresh air."

He considered her for a long moment, as if seeing beyond her facade. "We have known each other too long for pretence, Genevieve."

A blush stained her cheeks at her Christian name on his lips. "Forgive me," she said, a rueful twist to her mouth. "I find myself… overwhelmed by it all. By the crush, the noise, the expectations—" Her voice hitched. To her mortification, her eyes burned with tears.

In a heartbeat, he closed the distance between them and took her hands in his. "There is no need to explain, not to me." His thumbs traced gentle circles against her skin, his touch an anchor amidst the storm of her emotions. "I understand what it is to feel… adrift. Out of place in a world that demands so much."

The compassion in his voice threatened to undo her. She blinked back tears, afraid to meet his gaze and reveal the depths of her vulnerability.

"Look at me," he whispered.

Steeling herself, she did. And there, in the warm brown of his eyes, she found solace.

"You are stronger than you know," he continued, "braver and brighter than any of them can imagine. Do not let their expectations dim your light."

A tear slipped free, but she smiled. "How is it you always know just what to say?"

"Because I see you," he said. "The real you. Not what they want you to be, but who you are meant to become. I am sorry for what happened before you went to Rome. I am truly sorry."

Her heart swelled, overflowing with gratitude—and something more, a nascent tendril of hope. Perhaps in this new world, there was a place where she could be herself. Where she was known, and loved for who she was.

She squeezed his hands. "Thank you."

He smiled, soft and true. "You are most welcome."

Genevieve took a deep breath and squared her shoulders, gathering her composure. Mordesley was right—she was stronger than she knew. Braver and brighter than any of them could imagine.

She would not let their expectations dim her light.

Chapter Two

Sebastian strode through the manicured gardens, gravel crunching beneath his boots as he sought solitude from the inane chatter inside. The annual Astor ball was always insufferably dull, but this year had proved particularly tedious.

He paused by the marble fountain, its gentle splashing a balm to his restlessness. Since inheriting the title of Marquess three years prior, his patience for these frivolous social affairs had worn thin. They were a necessity to maintain appearances, but oh how he chafed at the constraints.

Leaning against the fountain's edge, Sebastian closed his eyes and inhaled the sweet floral scents wafting on the breeze. For a moment, he could pretend he was far away from the glittering cage of the ton and its crushing expectations.

The illusion was short-lived. Footsteps on the gravel announced the arrival of Lord Aynslie, an elderly peer with a predilection for lecturing his juniors.

"There you are, Mordesley," Aynslie blustered. "You must return inside directly. Several prominent families have arrived, and it is important that you be there to greet them."

Sebastian stifled a sigh. "Of course. I shall be along presently."

Aynslie harrumphed. "See that you make haste. I understand the St. Claires have just returned from an extended stay abroad. You were acquainted with the daughters as children, I believe?"

Sebastian stiffened. The St. Claires? After all these years abroad, could it be...?

"Yes," he said carefully. "Though it has been some time since I had the pleasure." Five years, in truth. Not since that summer, and the duel that had driven the St. Claires from England.

A familiar ache twisted in his chest. Lady Genevieve had always held a special place in his memories. Quick of wit and spirited of temper, she met him measure for measure. Until youthful passion and rash impulses ruined everything.

Aynslie was still talking. "Best make a good impression now that they have returned. Especially on the elder daughter. She is past marriageable age already, poor thing. Though I hear the younger girl is more than fair to look at."

Sebastian clenched his jaw. How dare this pompous fool refer to Genevieve in such a manner? He knew nothing of the clever brightness of her eyes, the sweet curve of her smile. She deserved far more than to be judged and dismissed so casually.

"If you will excuse me, my lord, I should make haste as you suggest," he forced out through gritted teeth. Aynslie nodded approvingly as Sebastian strode past him back towards the party.

His heart pounded as he entered the glaringly bright ballroom, every sense primed for a glimpse of chestnut curls or flashing hazel eyes. The crowd eddied around him, a blur of silk and supercilious smiles. Still, there was no sign of the St. Claire sisters.

Then, a ripple of awareness in the room. Heads turned; a chorus of whispers broke out. Through the parting crowd Sebastian glimpsed two young women in elegant gowns, one blonde and smiling, the other brunette with her gaze downcast. His pulse stuttered.

Genevieve. After all these years, still just as lovely. Her chin lifted and her eyes met his across the distance. Time seemed to slow. He saw the flicker of recognition in her guarded expression. Saw the softening of her mouth and quickening of her breath.

In that endless moment, the gulf of years between them vanished. He was just a man, and she just a woman, their hearts drawn together as though fate itself had intervened.

Then she looked away, the spell broken. Reality returned in a rush of noise and glare. But nothing could erase what he had glimpsed in her eyes. Possibility still remained.

Sebastian stood taller, imbued with new purpose. The past could not be rewritten, but the future lay unscribed. If he could just win Genevieve's forgiveness, perhaps they might yet find happiness together. A chance to redeem the mistakes of youth.

He would be patient and humble himself before her. Prove he was not the reckless boy who had hurt her, but a man of honour and integrity worthy of her faith. It would not be quick or easy, he knew. But she was worth any effort, any price. And for the first time in forever, hope flickered inside him once more.

Sebastian lingered on the fringes of the party, tracking Genevieve's movements while trying to appear nonchalant. He watched as she glided through the crowds, greeting acquaintances old and new, the consummate lady once more. Yet there was a restraint to her manner that had not been there before, a wariness in her eyes that pained him.

When Lord Daniels approached and asked her to dance, jealousy twisted hot and sharp in Sebastian's gut. He had no claim over Genevieve now, he knew that. But the sight of her in another man's arms stirred a possessiveness he had not anticipated.

As the music swelled, he was struck anew by how perfectly they moved together. The graceful sweep of her neck as she laughed at something Daniels said, the elegant poise of her frame as she twirled. Sebastian's fingers twitched with the muscle memory of having held her thus, intimately close. Yet now a distance yawned between them, one he feared could never be bridged.

The dance ended, and Sebastian watched with bated breath as Daniels escorted Genevieve off the floor. He leaned into whisper something Sebastian was too far away to hear. Annoyance flashed across her features, there and gone. Then she was gliding away, Daniels forgotten.

In that brief unguarded moment, Sebastian saw the Genevieve of old shine through. Quick-witted, sharp-tongued, too clever by half. He ached to speak with her again, to draw out that vibrant spirit once more. But he knew he must tread carefully. She had built walls around her heart, and he could not blame her.

As the night deepened, Sebastian wrestled with how to approach her. The gulf between who they were and who they had been seemed a vast and perilous expanse. How could he span such a distance?

The answer came as he watched Genevieve slip away to the balcony alone, as was her habit when a social occasion grew oppressive. Heart pounding, Sebastian made his decision. He would speak with her plainly and from the heart. No pretences, no flirtations. If there was to be hope for them, it must be founded on truth.

Sebastian found Genevieve alone on the balcony, gazing up at the night sky. He hesitated for a moment, unsure if he should approach. But seeing her withdraw from the festivities had sparked his concern.

Steeling himself, he walked over to her. "There you are. I was hoping to find you alone."

Genevieve startled at the sound of his voice, then turned to face him. "My lord. To what do I owe the pleasure?"

"You seemed distressed earlier. I wanted to ensure you were well." Sebastian kept his tone gentle, hoping she would sense his sincerity.

"How very kind." Her words were polite, but there was a wariness in her eyes that pained him. "'Tis nothing, merely the heat of the ballroom. I required a breath of fresh air."

Sebastian studied her closely, seeing past her façade. "We have known each other too long for pretence, Genevieve."

A blush rose in her cheeks at the use of her Christian name. "Forgive me. I find myself...overwhelmed by it all. By the crush, the noise, the expectations—" Her voice hitched, and she blinked rapidly.

His chest ached at the turmoil she was too proud to fully reveal. Acting on instinct, he closed the distance between them and took her hands in his. "There is no need to explain, not to me." He stroked his thumbs over her knuckles soothingly. "I understand what it is to feel... adrift. Out of place in a world that demands so much."

She took a shaky breath, still not meeting his eyes. Sebastian could sense her struggle, torn between maintaining her composure and accepting the comfort he offered.

"Look at me," he urged gently.

Finally, she lifted her gaze to his. The vulnerability he saw there made his breath catch.

"You are stronger than you know," he told her. "Braver and brighter than any of them can imagine."

A single tear escaped down her cheek, but her lips curved in a tremulous smile. "How is it you always know just what to say?"

"Because I see you. The real you." He hoped she could hear the sincerity in his words. "Not what they want you to be, but who you are meant to become."

Her eyes shimmered with some unspoken emotion. Then she gave his hands a gentle squeeze. "Thank you."

Though brief, the exchange felt like a minor triumph. Walls between them had cracked, if not crumbled completely. But it was a start. The rest, he knew, depended on Genevieve and the fragility of hope.

Sebastian watched Genevieve walk back into the ballroom, his palms still tingling from the warmth of her hands. Their first real conversation in years had been brief, but it left his mind spinning with possibility.

He had glimpsed behind her polished exterior to the vulnerability she tried so hard to conceal. It awoke in him an almost forgotten urge to comfort and protect her, as he had once done long ago. Before passion and foolishness had ruined the easy affection between them.

But the past could not be undone. Sebastian sighed, turning to gaze out over the shadowed gardens. Genevieve was not that girl anymore, nor was he the reckless youth who had callously broken her heart. The gulf of years had changed them both.

Yet in her eyes, he had seen echoes of the lively, quick-witted girl who had so often matched his wit and will as children. She was weary of the glittering facade now, much as he had become. They were kindred spirits adrift in a strange new world that demanded much and promised little.

If she would permit him back into her life, perhaps they could find anchorage in each other once more. Not as reckless youths grasping at passion, but as two world-weary souls seeking connection amidst the artifice. It would not be quick or easy, he knew. But she was worth every effort.

Squaring his shoulders, Sebastian left the balcony. The ballroom was stifling and cloying, but he would endure it. Watching for another chance to speak with Genevieve, to slowly rebuild what had been lost. He prayed she felt the fragile new bond between them and would give him the chance to strengthen it. Time would tell, but for now, hope flickered anew.

Chapter Three

The next several hours passed in a blur of curtsies and polite conversation. Genevieve greeted acquaintances old and new, careful to observe each nuance of etiquette. Though the rules of propriety still felt foreign on her tongue, she navigated them with newfound grace, buoyed by Mordesley's confidence in her abilities.

When Lord Avery approached to pay his respects, Genevieve greeted him with a warm smile. "It is wonderful to see you again, my lord."

"The pleasure is mine, Lady Genevieve." His eyes gleamed with interest. "You are looking as lovely as ever. Rome seems to have agreed with you."

"You are too kind." She inclined her head. "I must admit, however, it feels good to be home."

"London has missed your radiant presence," he said, taking her hand and pressing a kiss to her knuckles. "The season will be all the brighter for your return."

Genevieve blinked, startled by the overt compliment. Before she could muster a response, Lord Avery glanced up and released her hand. She followed his gaze to find Mordesley watching them, an unreadable expression on his face. Her stomach fluttered at the intensity of his regard.

Lord Avery cleared his throat. "If you will excuse me, Lady Genevieve, I should pay my respects to your mother."

"Of course," she said faintly. As he walked away, she looked to Mordesley, who had started toward her with feline grace. Her heart raced in anticipation of their meeting.

Perhaps she had found her place after all.

Sebastian Mordesley stopped before her and bowed. "Lady Genevieve. It is a pleasure to see you again."

His formal tone was at odds with the warmth in his eyes. Genevieve curtsied, a smile teasing at the corners of her lips. "The pleasure is mine, Lord Mordesley." Genevieve knew she must act like this was the first-time seeing Sebastian again for those that may be watching; the balcony's interlude may be seen as scandalous if anyone knew.

Straightening, he glanced around the ballroom. "London society has been much duller in your absence. I hope you do not intend to deprive us of your company again anytime soon."

"If it were up to me, I would not dream of it," she said, meeting his gaze. "However, my parents' wishes must come before my own."

"As is only proper." His lips quirked. "Though I doubt they wish for you to be unhappy. Perhaps we should form an alliance to keep you here, where you belong."

Genevieve laughed, a surge of affection swelling in her chest. How she had missed his teasing humour and quiet understanding. "I appreciate your concern for my happiness, my lord, but I must defer to my parents' judgment in this matter."

"Very well." He bowed his head in acquiescence. "I shall have to content myself with enjoying your company this evening."

"I hope I shall not disappoint."

"Impossible," he said softly, eyes glinting with unspoken promise.

A blush crept into her cheeks as she dropped her gaze. The rustle of silk and a subtle shift in the air warned her of his nearness. She looked up to find him leaning close, his breath warm against her ear.

"It is good to have you back, Genevieve."

Heart pounding, she watched him straighten and offer his arm. She placed her hand on the fine wool of his jacket, keenly aware of the strength and warmth beneath.

As they moved into the swirl of dancers, the familiar scents and sounds of a London ballroom enveloped her. But it was the presence of the man beside her, and the knowledge of being where she belonged, that made the occasion perfect.

That evening, as Genevieve prepared for bed in the familiar comfort of her old room, a sense of displacement crept over her. Through the open windows came the faint sounds of London at night—the clip-clop of horses' hooves, the rumble of carriages, and the occasional shout of a night watchman.

So different from the rhythms of Rome, with its ancient stones and fountains, and quiet nights under open skies. She missed the freedom of wandering the city with Georgina, exploring its hidden treasures and making secret discoveries of their own.

Here, there were rules to follow and expectations to meet. Propriety was paramount, and a woman's worth depended on her conduct and connections. Genevieve knew she should feel content in the familiarity of home, and grateful for the opportunities now afforded to her. Yet part of her longed to cast off the trappings of society and escape into the night, as she once had without a care.

With a sigh, she turned from the window and began brushing her hair. She must adapt to this new reality yet hold fast to the parts of herself that made her feel most alive. There had to be a way to navigate the complex web of London society on her own terms, even if she had not quite discerned it yet.

* * *

The next morning, Genevieve sought out her mother in the drawing room. Lady Penelope sat by the window, gazing out at the bustle of carriages and pedestrians passing by. She turned with a warm smile as Genevieve entered, her keen eyes betraying a hint of concern.

"Did you sleep well, my dear?" she asked. "I know how the excitement and nerves can wear on one upon returning to Town."

Genevieve nodded, taking a seat beside her mother. "Well enough. Though

I confess my thoughts were restless." She paused, wondering how best to frame her questions. Lady Penelope placed a gentle hand on her arm, her expression softening in understanding.

"You must not worry so, Genevieve. You are more than prepared to face society again, and we shall guide your steps as needed."

"It is not worry that plagues me, precisely," Genevieve said slowly. "More a longing for the freedom I found in Rome. A wish that I might live less bound by the rules of propriety and discover who I am meant to become in my own time."

Lady Penelope's brow creased in concern. "My dear girl, you know as well as I that a young woman of your station has certain duties to fulfil. While abroad we allowed you certain liberties, here in London your conduct and connections shall determine your worth." Her tone was gentle yet firm, leaving no room for argument.

Genevieve swallowed hard against the lump forming in her throat. She had known this would be her mother's response, yet part of her had hoped Lady Penelope might understand.

"Of course, Mama," she said softly. "There shan't be a repeat of the Bourbon's garden party."

"Yes, ideally you would stay away from horses. If you cannot, at least ride them side saddle or as part of a carriage team." Lady Penelope glared at her daughter.

Though she kept her expression serene, inside Genevieve felt torn in two. The path before her was clear, yet her heart yearned for another way. She would play her part in society and secure her future, all while guarding the wildness within that made her feel alive. It would not be an easy balance to strike, but for now, it was the only choice she had.

The next morning, Genevieve paid a call on her dear friend Lady Amelia Hawthorne. Since their days playing make-believe amongst the embroidered cushions in the nursery, Amelia had proven a stalwart confidante. Her playful spirit and penchant for mischief were a tonic against the strictures of society.

Amelia greeted Genevieve with an enthusiastic embrace that smelled comfortingly of lilac water and lemon Verbena. Linking her arm through

Genevieve's, she led them to the sunny morning room.

"Come, sit. Tell me everything!" Amelia said, practically pushing Genevieve into a chair. "I've been absolutely famished for details of your grand adventures in Rome. Your letters told of amazing things, but I feel there was so much more! What were the Lords like? You never told me why you left! "

Genevieve smiled indulgently at her friend's exuberance as she settled into the chintz-covered chair. "Oh! I will, but first…" She recounted the previous day's conversation with her mother, laying bare the conflicted tangle of her emotions. Amelia listened intently, absentmindedly pleating and un-pleating the skirt of her muslin gown.

When Genevieve finished, Amelia grasped her hand, green eyes flashing. "Stuff and nonsense. Do not let the old dragons cow you into conforming, my dear. We shall simply have to be clever in how we manoeuvre society this season." A conspiratorial grin lit her face. "I happen to excel at ingenious schemes, as you well know."

Genevieve couldn't help returning her friend's infectious smile, feeling her spirits lift. Dearest Amelia always knew how to make the best of things and turn the most mundane events into grand adventures. With Amelia by her side, perhaps the looming Season would not seem so daunting after all.

"You're right, as always," Genevieve said. "If anyone can help me navigate the perils of the Ton unscathed, it is you."

Amelia let out a peal of laughter. "The perils of the Ton! What a delightful turn of phrase. I will warn you though several of the young men we watched as girls now have a reputation as rakes. Including Lord Mordesley, whom I know you were quite partial to." Genevieve made a face. "Now tell me…"

As Amelia chattered on animatedly about the upcoming social season, Genevieve felt a swell of gratitude for this truest of friends. Together they would face the complexities of London society on their own terms, propriety be damned. She had made her resolution, and nothing would stand in her way. The news that Sebastian was considered a rake did not surprise her. His past actions had proved him capable. She felt affection for him, and his words at the ball had made her think he felt similar, however, doubts began to creep in. What if it had all been part of an act? Confusion reigned in her head.

* * *

The sun dipped below the horizon, its golden light filtering through the trees of Hyde Park. Genevieve inhaled the scent of lilacs as she strolled along the winding path, her gloved hand resting on her sister Georgina's arm.

"The weather has been sublime this week, has it not?" Georgina said. "Perfect weather for our afternoon constitutionals."

"Indeed." Genevieve gazed at the other ladies promenading in their finery, a vision of silk and lace under the dusky sky. Though she kept pace with Georgina, her thoughts wandered as they often did during these walks. Part of her chafed at the strict rules of propriety that dictated even the smallest details of her life, longing to break free of the shackles of polite society. Yet she knew it was her duty to make a suitable match, as her mother never ceased to remind her.

Georgina glanced at her with a frown. "You seem distracted today, Genevieve. Is something amiss?"

Genevieve forced a smile, pushing her restless thoughts aside. "Of course not. Simply admiring the view on this fine evening."

Her sister studied her, a flicker of concern in her eyes, but after a moment she turned her gaze forward once more. "We should return home soon. You know how Mother frets if we are out after dark."

"You are right, of course." Though the sun had nearly vanished beyond the horizon, its warmth still lingered. Genevieve breathed in the fragrance of flowers and new leaves once more, imprinting it on her memory. No matter the constraints of her life, at least she had these quiet moments.

With a rustle of silk, she and Georgina started back down the path toward home. The park was emptying out now, the last golden rays of sunset caressing the quiet lawns. Genevieve walked in silence, finding solace in the stillness. Whatever her fate, she would cling to these fleeting moments of peace for as long as she could.

Genevieve tucked a stray curl behind her ear, gazing out at the dusky silhouettes of trees against the darkening sky. The gravel path stretched before her, lit by the soft glow of lanterns. Most of the ton had already departed for the evening, leaving the park nearly deserted.

A faint strain of music drifted to her, and she paused, tilting her head to listen. The melody was unfamiliar, complex, and haunting. She searched the shadows until she spied a lone figure seated on a bench, leaning over an instrument that glinted in the half-light.

"Do you recognise the piece?" Georgina asked, coming up beside her.

Genevieve shook her head. "I cannot quite place it. The style seems almost Baroque, yet there is something else…" Her voice trailed off as the man looked up, pale eyes meeting hers across the distance. A shiver of recognition ran down her spine.

Sebastian. Of course, it would be him.

Heat rose in her cheeks as she recalled their last encounter, a mix of attraction and annoyance swirling within her. Why did this man have such an effect on her composure? She straightened her shoulders, willing her expression into one of cool indifference.

He set the violin aside and stood, making his way over to them with languid grace. "Lady Genevieve, Lady Georgina, what a pleasant surprise." His voice was like velvet, soft and sinuous. "I see you have an ear for the violin as well as poetry."

Genevieve lifted her chin. "We happened to overhear you. I would not call that a particular talent."

One corner of his mouth curled upward. "As you say." His gaze lingered on hers, a subtle challenge in those pale eyes. "May I walk you home? The paths can be dangerous after dark."

She hesitated, torn between refusal and curiosity. When had she become so indecisive in this man's presence? With an inward sigh, she inclined her head. "Thank you, Lord Mordesley. We would appreciate an escort."

His smile deepened; satisfaction etched into every line of his face. Genevieve frowned, annoyed at herself for rising to his bait yet again. Sebastian fell into step beside her, and the three of them started down the path at a leisurely pace.

The path wound through shadows and starlight, empty at this late hour. An awkward silence fell over them, broken only by the crunch of gravel beneath their feet.

Genevieve glanced at Sebastian from the corner of her eye, noticing the way the dim light softened his angular features. He walked with his hands behind his back, cutting a striking figure in his dark greatcoat.

She looked away, a flush rising in her cheeks. Why did he insist on discomposing her at every turn?

"You play beautifully," she said, grasping for a neutral topic of conversation. "I did not know you had talent with the violin."

"Thank you," he said. "Music has always been a passion of mine. Do you play any instruments yourself, Lady Genevieve?"

"The pianoforte," she said. "Though not with any particular skill."

"I find that difficult to believe." His tone held a teasing note. "A woman of your talents must excel at all pursuits."

Genevieve bit back a retort, annoyed at the flattery. Did he hope to win her favour through insincere compliments? She would not give him the satisfaction of a response.

Silence fell again. Out of the corner of her eye, she noticed Sebastian watching her. Waiting, no doubt, for her to rise to his bait once more.

She kept her gaze fixed ahead, a muscle twitching in her jaw. He could stand there in smug silence all night for all she cared. She would not give him the pleasure of her annoyance.

The tension built between them, as palpable as the chill in the air. By the time they reached her front gate, it had coalesced into a strange ache in the pit of her stomach.

Sebastian bid them a crisp goodnight, but even after he had disappeared into the shadows, Genevieve remained unsettled.

What was it about this man that provoked her so? And why did their every encounter leave her more confused than the last?

Shaking her head, she followed Georgina inside. The warmth of the foyer did little to ease the strange disquiet in her heart. Sebastian's effect on her was as maddening as ever, like a tune she could not get out of her head.

Chapter Four

The next day, Genevieve found her thoughts drifting to Sebastian once more as she strolled through Hyde Park with Georgina. She scolded herself for allowing him to occupy her mind, but it was no use. Like a persistent shadow, his memory followed her wherever she went.

"You've been rather quiet today," Georgina said. "Is something amiss?"

Genevieve forced a smile. "Merely lost in thought."

"Ah. Penny for them?"

She shook her head. "It's nothing of import."

But even as she denied it, her gaze scanned the park. And there, across the path, she found him at last—the subject of her restless thoughts. Sebastian.

He stood beneath the shade of an oak tree, one hand clasped behind his back as he conversed with another gentleman. His face was half-hidden by the brim of his hat, but she would have recognised his proud, upright bearing anywhere.

As if sensing her gaze, Sebastian glanced up. For a single, breathless moment, their eyes met from across the lawn. A spark of familiar heat kindled in her chest at the sight of his smouldering stare.

Then he looked away again, leaving her cheeks aflame with colour. Her heart pounded as though she had just run a mile, not merely exchanged a glance.

"There now," Georgina said knowingly. "I believe I've found the source of your distraction."

Genevieve pressed a hand to her chest as if she could quell the riotous beat of her heart through sheer force of will. "Do not be absurd," she said, but the sharpness of her tone betrayed her.

Georgina's answering smile only deepened her embarrassment. Merciful heavens, was she truly so transparent? "Let us sit for a while and admire the view."

Before she could protest further, a shadow fell over them. "Lady Genevieve. Lady Georgina." Sebastian's voice, smooth as silk, caressed her senses. "What a pleasant surprise."

Genevieve swallowed and summoned a polite smile, hoping it did not appear as strained as it felt. "Lord Mordesley." She dipped into a curtsy, grateful for the excuse to hide her flushed cheeks. "The pleasure is ours."

When she rose again, Sebastian's gaze lingered on her face, his own expression unreadable. Her heart performed a clumsy somersault.

"May I join you?" he asked.

Georgina, bless her, came to Genevieve's rescue. "We would be delighted to have your company."

Sebastian settled onto the bench beside Genevieve, leaning back and crossing one ankle over his knee in a posture of studied ease. The faint scent of sandalwood and bergamot teased at her senses, as intoxicating as any French perfume.

"The gardens seem to have drawn most of the Ton today," Sebastian observed. "An unseasonably warm day, is it not?"

"Quite lovely," Genevieve managed. She kept her hands folded tightly in her lap; afraid he might notice their trembling if she did not.

"Have you been enjoying the exhibits in the garden?" he asked. "I found the sculptures particularly inspiring."

At the mention of art, Genevieve's nerves eased. Here was a topic she could discuss with confidence. "Yes, there are several fine pieces. The marble Aphrodite especially struck me. The artist captured her grace and beauty admirably."

Sebastian's mouth curved. "A keen observation. I can see you have an eye for art as well as music."

A spark of pleasure lit within her at the compliment. "And you, my lord, seem to have an interest in both."

"As do you," he said smoothly. "We have more in common than you realise, Lady Genevieve."

His words, soft as a caress, kindled a warmth in her cheeks that had little to do with embarrassment. For the first time since her return, she sensed the attraction between them was not one-sided. The realisation left her breathless with mingled delight and apprehension.

Georgina, who had been following the exchange with evident amusement, rose to her feet. "If you will excuse me, I see an acquaintance I must greet."

Genevieve's eyes widened in mute protest, but her sister had already whisked away, leaving her alone with Sebastian on the bench.

Heart pounding, she searched for something to say to break the sudden silence. But Sebastian spoke first, his voice edged with wry humour.

"It seems I have been abandoned to your mercy, my lady."

The tension eased from her shoulders, and she laughed. "Then you have nothing to fear, sir, so long as you avoid discussions of embroidery or the latest fashion in bonnets."

"I shall keep that in mind," Sebastian said gravely, though his eyes glinted with concealed mirth.

Emboldened by his teasing manner, Genevieve tilted her head and regarded him through the veil of her lashes. "And what topics would you suggest, Lord Mordesley, if we are to continue our conversation?"

Sebastian leaned back against the bench, shifting his posture to cross the other ankle over the other knee in a posture of relaxed indolence.

"We could discuss the latest novel to capture the imagination of the Ton, debate the merits of Gothic versus classical architecture, or argue whether science will ultimately prove the undoing of faith." He shrugged, a wry half-smile twisting his lips. "I leave the choice to you, Lady Genevieve. My interests are wide-ranging, and I find beauty in the discovery of a new perspective, no matter the subject."

His words conjured images of long, stimulating conversations by candle-light, full of laughter and lively exchanges that awoke her mind from its usual slumber. A longing rose inside her, sudden and sharp, for a partnership of true equals. One based not on duty or obligation but a meeting of minds and hearts.

Genevieve blinked, disconcerted by the strength of her fanciful imaginings. Though they had known each other well as children, she hardly knew this man, no matter his charm or intellect. Cautiousness dictated she guard her heart until she had a better sense of his character.

"You have a curious way of evoking grand ideas and then leaving the choice to execute them to your companion," she said, hoping to disguise the turbulent nature of her thoughts.

"And you have a curious way of perceiving both the subtlest nuance and the heart of the matter." Sebastian's gaze turned inward for a moment. "It is a rare gift, and one I find… intriguing."

Heat rose in her cheeks at the warmth in his tone and the way his eyes seemed to see beyond her practised facade of politeness. She looked away, watching a group of children chase each other around the park, their laughter ringing out in the golden light of late afternoon. Again, she was reminded of the sun dappled hallway, warm breath and that baritone saying 'intriguing'.

His next words were soft, meant for her ears alone. "Have I distressed you, Genevieve?"

She shook her head, then summoned a smile as she met his gaze. "No. You have simply given me something to think on."

Something indeed. She had the feeling her thoughts would be occupied with Sebastian long after they parted. And that both delighted and dismayed her.

Standing, they walked in silence for a time, Genevieve casting surreptitious glances at Sebastian as he observed the other park visitors. His features were finely sculpted, betraying a blend of intellect and worldliness few men possessed. She found herself wondering about the experiences that had shaped him, and what mysteries yet lay behind those perceptive eyes.

Her musings were interrupted by a trio of ladies passing by their hushed whispers carrying on the breeze.

"Did you hear? The Marquess Mordesley was seen leaving Lady Jane Rowland's townhouse just before dawn."

"Again? He is utterly incorrigible."

"They say his appetites are insatiable. However does he find the time for his parliamentary duties, let alone properly courting an eligible young lady?"

Genevieve's cheeks flamed at the implication, and she risked a glance at Sebastian to find his jaw clenched, a muscle twitching in his cheek. Her stomach sank as she considered the truth behind their gossip. Had her heart led her astray so quickly?

Sebastian slowed his steps, gaze sweeping the path ahead. "Forgive me, Lady Genevieve, but I find I have forgotten an important engagement. It was a pleasure having your company. I do hope we meet again."

Without waiting for a reply, he strode off in the direction of the street, leaving Genevieve staring after him in dismay. The rumours could not be ignored, and she berated herself for being so easily swayed by a handsome face and artful tongue.

Amelia had been right to warn her. Even if Sebastian Mordesley was not the rake society proclaimed him to be, he was obviously a man with secrets. And that was something her reputation could ill afford.

Genevieve quickened her steps to catch up with Georgina, who was strolling ahead without a care. How she envied her sister's blithe disregard for propriety and convention.

"Did you hear what those ladies were saying about Lord Mordesley?" Genevieve asked in a low voice as she drew up beside Georgina.

"I did." Georgina sighed. "It seems our mysterious Marquess is not so mysterious after all. Still, I do not put much stock in idle gossip and rumour."

"This was more than mere rumour," Genevieve said. "Did you not see how he reacted? He all but fled the moment those words were uttered."

"All I observed was a man in control of his emotions, as any gentleman would be."

Genevieve frowned, unconvinced. While her sister had always been too trusting and ready to see the good in others, Genevieve tended to err on the side of caution. And everything about Sebastian Mordesley screamed danger.

"Promise me you will not encourage his attentions," she said. "I do not wish to see you hurt or your reputation compromised by association."

Georgina's eyes widened. "Dearest sister, you cannot mean to forbid me from speaking with the man."

"I can and I shall if you do not give me your word," Genevieve said sharply.

Georgina stared at her for a long moment before nodding with reluctant acquiescence. "Very well. I shall steer clear of the mysterious Marquess if it will put your mind at ease."

Genevieve breathed a sigh of relief, the tightness in her chest easing. At least she had protected one heart from Sebastian Mordesley's dubious charms, even if she could not safeguard her own.

That evening, Genevieve sat by the fire in her bedchamber, a book lying forgotten in her lap as her thoughts drifted to Sebastian Mordesley. She had told herself it was concern for her sister's welfare that prompted her demand for Georgina to avoid the man. But if she were honest with herself, it was her own heart she feared would be imperilled if she were to see him again.

Against all reason, she found herself recalling the vivid blue of his eyes, the relaxed timbre of his voice, the effortless way he had engaged her in a lively debate over the merits of Wordsworth's poetry. Try as she might, she could not reconcile the charming companion she had encountered in the park with the dissolute rake of rumour and gossip, though his actions 5 years ago did not help his cause.

Genevieve pressed the heels of her hands against her temples, as if she could squeeze out the memory of him through sheer force. What a foolish, reckless impulse it had been to speak with him at all. She had been so captivated in the moment, but at what cost? Now her peace of mind was shattered, her thoughts in tumult.

With a sigh, she closed her book and rang for her maid. Best to retire early and hope that the arrival of a new day would bring clarity and composure. As her maid helped her prepare for bed, Genevieve steeled herself for the long hours ahead. The night would be sleepless, she feared, haunted by the spectre of Sebastian Mordesley and the questions that had no easy answers.

Her heart and her reason were at odds, and she could not yet tell which would emerge the victor.

The next morning dawned grey and gloomy, mirroring Genevieve's restless mood. She had managed little sleep, her mind chasing itself in circles until the first pale light of dawn crept into her room.

Now, as she gazed out the window at the steady rain, she felt more unsettled than ever. The day stretched before her, empty hours to be filled with doubt and indecision. She yearned to speak with someone who could offer guidance, a voice of reason that was not her own.

With sudden determination, Genevieve rang for her maid. "Please ask my mother if she will join me for tea this morning." Her mother was the most logical choice. Stern but loving, Lady Penelope would give her honest counsel and help her work through the tangle of emotions Sebastian Mordesley had left in his wake.

When her mother arrived, Genevieve poured the tea with a steady hand, marshalling her composure. Still, she could not meet her mother's gaze directly, staring instead into the depths of her teacup. How could she explain her encounter with the Marquess, much less the effect he had upon her? The words would not come, and an awkward silence stretched between them.

Lady Penelope set down her cup and reached for Genevieve's hands. "There is something troubling you, dear heart. I can see it plainly. Will you not share your cares with me?"

Genevieve swallowed hard against the lump in her throat. She had come this far; she could not falter now. Lifting her gaze at last, she confessed in a rush, "Mama, I have become reacquainted with the Marquess of Mordesley."

Lady Penelope's eyes widened. "The Marquess? My dear, whatever has he done to distress you so?"

"Nothing," Genevieve said hastily. "That is, he has done nothing improper. We merely conversed, and I found him quite charming."

"I see." Her mother studied her shrewdly. "But something about this encounter has unsettled you. What is it?"

Genevieve worried her lower lip. How could she explain the tumult of emotions that had gripped her since meeting Sebastian Mordesley again—the heady thrill of witty conversation, the strange vulnerability she had felt under the intensity of his gaze, the longing to know more of him despite the ominous rumours that trailed in his wake?

She took a steadying breath. "Mama, I fear I have developed an interest in the Marquess that can only lead to heartache. You know as well as I his reputation as a rake and a rogue. Any attachment between us would be impossible."

"His reputation may be exaggerated, as is so often the case," Lady Penelope said gently. "The only way to know for certain is through personal acquaintance."

"But at what cost?" Genevieve cried. "If even half of what is said about him is true, he could ruin me."

"My dear, you must not let idle gossip and speculation rule your judgment." Her mother gave her hands a comforting squeeze. "The Marquess's character is not so easily defined. There may be hidden depths that belie his reputation. If you feel a true connection, it may be worth pursuing to find the truth of him—with proper caution and discretion, of course."

"You cannot be serious!" Genevieve stared at her mother in disbelief, torn between gratitude for her counsel and dismay at the prospect of throwing caution to the wind where Sebastian Mordesley was concerned. Her mother had always been a voice of prudence and propriety. How could she suggest taking such a risk now?

Lady Penelope smiled gently at her shock. "My dear, I have always advised you to follow your heart but to do so wisely. That is my counsel now. Be wary of the Marquess, but do not close your heart to him without due consideration. Therein lies your best hope of finding happiness and avoiding regret. That being said, do not close your heart off to others who may be looking. I've had several enquiries and some are just as good and more suitable than the Marquess."

With that, her mother pressed a kiss to Genevieve's forehead and took her leave, leaving behind a piece of advice as troubling as it was liberating. Genevieve was more uncertain than ever- but also more determined to discover the truth of Sebastian Mordesley, if she dared. "But mother."

Genevieve whispered to the closed door. "It was Sebastian that Gregory duelled."

Chapter Five

Sebastian strode through the manicured gardens, the gravel path crunching beneath his boots. Though the sun shone brightly overhead, his thoughts were murky with disquiet.

Another aimless day spent charming the ton and playing the rake when his spirit felt anything but light. The facade was wearing thin, and the emptiness behind it threatened to swallow him whole.

These melancholy moods had become more frequent of late, though he took pains to hide them. Since returning to London and inheriting his title several years prior, he felt adrift and without purpose. The meaningless diversions of society could not fill the void for long.

A gust of wind stirred the trees, leaves rustling overhead. Sebastian paused beside a marble fountain, trailing his fingers in the cool water. Unbidden, his thoughts turned to Lady Genevieve St. Claire, as they so often did these days.

From their first encounter after her return from abroad, she had captured his interest in a way no other woman had. Quick-witted and unconventional, with an alluring air of mystery about her. He sensed hidden depths beneath her polished exterior, a wildness straining to break free.

Not that he had any right to her confidences, or her affections. Their shared history was fraught enough without adding romantic entanglements to the mix. Still, he found himself wishing they could recapture the easy friendship of childhood, before youthful passions and hot blood had destroyed it all.

Sebastian grimaced, shaking off these idle thoughts. Genevieve occupied far too much of his mind lately. She was a distraction he could ill afford. There were wrongs from his past that must be made right before he could think of indulging his own desires.

His path was clear, if difficult. Seek atonement through dutiful service to his family name and redemption in the eyes of society. Prove he could reform his ways and become the honourable gentleman he was raised to be. Then perhaps the emptiness inside might be filled.

With a weary sigh, Sebastian turned toward home. The sun still shone, and birds sang overhead, but the gardens seemed to mock his melancholy mood. The future loomed ahead, filled only with tedium.

Unless a certain chestnut-haired lady might consent to brighten it. Despite his misgivings, a treacherous spark of anticipation flickered in Sebastian's breast. Wherever Lady Genevieve was concerned, propriety often fell by the wayside.

If she would permit him back into her world, perhaps they could find the way forward together. It was a dangerous notion, but suddenly the coming days did not seem quite so bleak. Sighing he made his way to White's Gentleman's club, even men must keep up appearances.

The fire crackled merrily in the hearth of the ornate drawing room, casting flickering shadows across the distinguished gentlemen gathered within. Sebastian reclined in a leather wingback armchair, glass of brandy in hand, only half listening as Lord Drurie regaled the group with his latest tale of romantic conquest.

"So, there we were, in the pantry, her skirts hiked up to her waist, when who should happen upon us but the housekeeper!" Drurie exclaimed, eliciting raucous laughter from the others. Even Sebastian could not suppress an amused chuckle.

Lord Westerford, well into his cups, raised his glass in an unsteady toast. "To Drurie's insatiable appetites! Not even the most vigilant of housekeepers can thwart you."

"Here, here!" the men cheered.

Drurie preened, smoothing a hand over his ivory satin waistcoat. "As I always say, the only locks I cannot pick are those guarding a virtuous woman's chastity." He winked. "And precious few of those left in London."

More guffaws greeted this remark. Sebastian took another sip of brandy, the alcohol leaving a bitter aftertaste on his tongue. Once, he would have heartily joined in their merriment and boasted of his own romantic feats. But such pastimes had lost their appeal, leaving him weary and disillusioned.

Westerford leaned forward with a leer. "Come now, Mordesley, you've been uncharacteristically quiet. Surely London's most notorious rake has some tale to share? Which lovely lady has caught the great marquess's eye of late?"

Sebastian contemplated his glass. There was only one woman who occupied his thoughts these days, but he would not sully Genevieve's good name by involving her in such crude banter.

"Alas, my wandering days appear to be behind me," he said lightly. "It seems I make a better politician than Casanova."

"Hell's bells, don't tell me you mean to reform!" Drurie cried. "London's ladies will be bereft without you to warm their beds. Lady Constance will surely wither without your attentions!" Several of the men snickered.

"Let the man be," Lord Henry chided. Nearly twice their age, he had always acted as a kind of mentor to Sebastian and his peers, offering wisdom and measured counsel. "There comes a time when youthful passions cool and a man longs for more meaningful pursuits."

"Meaningful pursuits? At our age?" Drurie snorted into his brandy. "What could be more meaningful than the thrill of the chase and the company of beautiful women?"

Sebastian swirled the dark liquid in his glass, contemplating Henry's words. Was that truly what plagued him of late? A restlessness, a longing for something beyond these hollow pleasures and rakish pursuits? Try as he might, he could not deny a shift within himself, subtle but persistent.

"Do not discount the value of settling down, building a legacy," Henry said mildly. "Sharing one's life with a worthy partner. Our good marquess may have the right of it, looking to the future rather than dwelling in the pastimes of youth."

The other men grumbled and scoffed at this, but Sebastian pondered Henry's advice. It was not the first time the older gentleman had gently hinted he was destined for more meaningful things.

"Enough dreary talk of the future!" Drurie declared. "Let us speak instead of the fairer sex and their delightful attributes. Come, Mordesley, you must regale us with details of your latest paramours. It has been ages since we heard tale of your amorous adventures."

Sebastian hesitated. He had no wish to invent vulgar escapades to satisfy their expectations. But perhaps he could steer the conversation in a more thoughtful direction.

"If you wish to speak of women," he began slowly, "might I propose a philosophical debate instead? Let us discuss not only their charms, but their hearts and minds. Their hopes, fears and desires."

The others stared at him as though he had sprouted a second head. Sebastian shifted under the scrutiny but held firm. "You may think me mad, but how well do we truly understand women, for all our...experience? We appreciate only their physical beauty, not the depth of their spirits. Perhaps it is time we expanded our views."

"Hear, hear," Henry seconded approvingly.

Drurie blinked rapidly before bursting into laughter. "Saints preserve us, Mordesley's gone soft! What's next, writing romantic sonnets and picking wildflowers?"

Westerford joined in Drurie's mockery, the two making exaggerated kissing noises. Sebastian kept his expression neutral, refusing to be baited. After a moment, their laughter died down.

Drurie shook his head. "What nonsense is this? Women aren't interested in poetry or philosophical notions. They care only for fortune and fashion, securing a wealthy match before their looks fade. Isn't that right, Westerford?"

"Quite so," Westerford agreed. "And they will gladly exchange their virtue for gifts and lavish entertainments. Their hearts and minds are ruled by fickle whims and base appetites, not lofty sentiment."

The others nodded, but Sebastian noted Henry's frown of disapproval.

Before either could respond, Drurie continued pontificating. "We gentlemen must maintain a certain mystique, a little mystery and danger, to keep women enthralled." He jabbed a finger at Sebastian. "That is why you have always had such success with the fairer sex. You understand how to play the game."

Sebastian stared into the dying embers, regret settling heavily upon him. Once, he had believed as Drurie did, dallying with women's affections out of boredom and vanity. But what had it truly gained him, other than a tarnished reputation? How much harm had his careless pastimes caused the ladies in question?

"Perhaps it is time to change the rules of the game," he said quietly. "To seek more meaningful unions, with womankind as helpmeets and partners, not merely playthings to be toyed with and discarded at will."

The others gaped at him in varying degrees of surprise and dismay. Lord Henry regarded Sebastian with dawning approbation. "You show wisdom beyond your years, my boy." He lifted his glass. "To the fairer sex, so often underestimated and misunderstood. May we educate ourselves in the art of appreciating both their beauties and their spirits."

After a moment, Drurie and Westerford begrudgingly raised their glasses in tribute as well. The conversation soon turned to other matters, but Sebastian's thoughts lingered on all they had discussed. It seemed his instincts had been correct - he had indeed outgrown the shallow hedonism of his youth. A restless longing for something more substantial, more meaningful, plagued him still. But what form might that take?

Marriage was out of the question, for he had long sworn off binding himself to any woman in that way. The fairer sex remained an enigma to him, their hearts unknowable and desires inscrutable. Even Genevieve, as fond as he was of her, surely saw him only as the scoundrel who had nearly ruined her and her brother. He hardly deserved her regard, much less her hand. No, a solitary future awaited him, one he had earned through his own youthful follies.

Unless… inspired by his discussion, Sebastian wondered if the key to unlocking the mysteries of the gentler sex might lie in increased familiarity. Much as Henry advocated, he required a better understanding of women's minds and wants, if he were to move beyond his checkered history to a more enlightened future.

He needed to observe ladies up close in their natural environment, free from all pretence. To converse with them unguardedly, share in their interests, win their confidences. And what better place to interact informally with the cream of society than a ball? Settling back in his chair, Sebastian resolved to host a lavish ball soon and take full advantage of the opportunity.

He would not attend merely for idle flirtation or gossip as in years past, but with an open mind and willingness to learn. If he made the effort, perhaps an honest discourse might develop, allowing him insight into the secret desires and dreams of the fairer sex. And who knew? With harmony and good faith, he might gain not only understanding, but true friendship - and more.

The fire slowly died to embers as the others drank and debated. But Sebastian's mind was alight with inspiration. For the first time in ages, he felt motivated by a sense of purpose. There was much to learn about the opposite sex, and about himself. This ball would mark the beginning of his education, and if he was very fortunate, bring him one step closer to piecing together the perplexing enigma that was womankind.

Chapter Six

A few days later, a cream-coloured invitation arrived on crisp vellum paper, its silver calligraphy gleaming in the morning light.

Genevieve stared at the elaborate detailing, her heart leaping into her throat. An invitation to a grand ball at Mordesley House. Sebastian was hosting a ball.

She traced the curling letters of her name with trembling fingers, a riot of emotions churning within her. Excitement and apprehension. Curiosity and doubt. Longing and fear.

Sebastian had not forgotten their encounter, it seemed. But was this invitation a gesture of interest or merely courtesy? She had no way of knowing for certain, though she suspected his motives were not easily discerned.

Genevieve sighed, weighing the ivory card in her hands as she considered her mother's counsel. This could be an opportunity to discover the truth of Sebastian Mordesley, if she dared to take the risk. But did she dare?

The whispers of his rakish reputation echoed in her memory, a warning she could not easily ignore. And yet…she found herself tempted to throw caution aside for one evening, if only to lose herself again in the charm and wit of his company.

To follow her heart or her good judgment? It was a choice fraught with uncertainty, but in the end, curiosity won out.

Genevieve penned her acceptance, pulse racing as she sealed her fate. She would attend the ball at Mordesley House, come what may. The truth of Sebastian Mordesley awaited her, for better or for worse. She only hoped she would not live to regret her decision.

The days crept by with agonizing slowness, each hour bringing Genevieve closer to the ball and the storm of emotions it evoked. Anticipation and anxiety warred ceaselessly within her breast, robbing her of sleep and appetite until she grew pale and wan.

Her mother noticed the change at once, eyeing her with concern over the breakfast table. "Are you unwell, Genevieve?" she asked. "You have scarcely touched your food and there are dark circles under your eyes."

Genevieve forced a smile, reaching for a piece of toast she had no desire to eat. "Merely restless, Mama. The excitement of the season is wearing on me, I suppose."

It was not a complete falsehood. The bustle of the London season did drain her at times, though that was not the cause of her distress now. But she could hardly confess the truth—not when it would only fuel her mother's disapproval and strengthen her campaign against Sebastian Mordesley.

"Hmm." Her mother did not seem entirely convinced, but let the matter drop, turning her attention to Georgina instead.

Genevieve breathed a quiet sigh of relief, pushing away her plate as her stomach churned with nerves. The ball was nigh upon her, and with it, the moment of truth she both craved and dreaded. Would the gossip prove true, or would she find in Sebastian a man of honour and integrity beneath the charming facade?

She would know soon enough. Tonight, her fate would be sealed—for better or for worse.

The day passed at a snail's pace, each hour ticking towards the ball like the fall of an executioner's axe. Genevieve found little reprieve from her anxiety, her thoughts chasing themselves in endless circles.

One moment, she was convinced Sebastian was precisely the sort of dishonourable rake she ought to avoid. The next, she recalled the intensity of his gaze, the keenness of his wit, and felt herself melting once more.

She hovered indecisively before her wardrobe, unable to settle on a gown. Did she wish to appear aloof or alluring? Modest or daring? Each choice felt fraught with meaning, as if the wrong outfit might seal her fate before she even descended the steps into the glittering ballroom.

At last, she selected a gown of ivory silk, hoping it struck a balance between innocence and allure. But in truth, she suspected the real test had little to do with any outward show. Tonight, she would look into Sebastian's eyes once more—and in that meeting, she would find her answer.

Lady Genevieve stood patiently as her lady's maid, Clara, laced up the back of her new ivory silk ballgown. The cool silk felt delightful against her skin as Clara tightened the ribbons of the corset underneath, pulling in her already slender waist.

"You look beautiful tonight, my lady," Clara said as she arranged the capped sleeves to fall just so off Lady Genevieve's shoulders.

Genevieve studied her reflection in the full length mirror. The ivory silk complemented her creamy complexion and chestnut hair, which was swept up in an elegant twist, exposing her long, graceful neck. Tiny pearl earrings adorned her ears and matched the teardrop pearl necklace resting above her collarbone.

She turned this way and that, admiring the way the gown draped perfectly over her curves. The rich ivory colour reminded her of fresh cream, pure and virginal. An image came to mind of a certain gentleman's reaction when he saw her in it, and a little flutter of anticipation rose in her chest.

"It's perfect," Genevieve declared. "You've outdone yourself, Clara."

Clara smiled proudly as she made a few last minute adjustments, fussing over imaginary wrinkles. Finally, she handed Genevieve her silk gloves and reticule.

"I hope you have a wonderful time tonight, my lady. You look every inch the belle of the ball."

Genevieve swept Clara a gracious smile. "Thank you, Clara. I shall be the envy of every girl there."

Checking her appearance one last time in the mirror, Genevieve glided out of her bedchamber and down the stairs, her gown trailing elegantly behind her. She was ready for the ball, and hoped the night would hold a magical encounter with a certain gentleman she longed to see again.

Her heart pounded as the carriage rolled up the gravel drive, lit by the golden glow of a hundred torches. The Mordesley estate was even grander than she had imagined, the ballroom within thronged with guests and alight with the bright gleam of chandeliers.

For a moment the grandeur and spectacle overwhelmed her senses, and she lingered near the entrance to gather her wits. But it was not the crush of people or the strains of the orchestra that unsettled her most.

Amidst the swirl of colour and sound, Sebastian was waiting, and her fate was soon to come. She scanned the room, searching for any sign of Sebastian's tall, imposing figure. But in the sea of lavish gowns and tailored coats, he remained elusive. "To think the host of the ball is not greeting his guests." Lady Penelope tisked. "Outrageous!"

With a deep breath, she steeled her nerves and descended the steps into the ballroom. At once she was surrounded by acquaintances offering greetings and eager to discuss the latest on-dits. She replied with a practiced smile, all the while peering over shoulders and around conversing groups, her heart quickening at each glimpse of a dark head or broad shoulder.

After a quarter hour of restless waiting, she began to despair of finding him. Perhaps he never intended to show at his own ball or had deliberately avoided an encounter to torment her. The thought stung more than she cared to admit.

Just then a familiar voice spoke at her elbow. "I was beginning to fear you would not come."

She turned to find Sebastian gazing down at her, a subtle smile playing about his lips. A rush of relief and trepidation flooded her senses. "My lord," she said, dipping into a curtsy. "How fortunate you are that I chose to grace your ball after all."

His smile deepened, crinkling the corners of his eyes. "Indeed. The fates have smiled on me tonight."

Heat rose in her cheeks, though she kept her tone light. "Let us hope your good fortune holds, my lord."

"I have never been one to trust in fortune alone," he said, his gaze intent upon her face. "The outcomes I desire most, I take into my own hands."

A nervous flutter stirred in her stomach at the implication behind his words. The moment of truth had arrived at last. She searched his face, looking for any sign that might guide her decision. But in the end, she realised the truth had always been clear. She could no more resist him than she could her own heart.

She drew a steadying breath and lifted her chin. "Then I suggest you seize this opportunity, my lord, before fortune decides to snatch it away."

His eyes widened briefly before a smile of pure delight curved his lips. "My dear Genevieve." He offered his arm, which she accepted readily, a giddy joy rising within her. As they entered the dancefloor together, a hush fell over the crowd. All eyes turned to the pair, and a swell of whispers rose in their wake, the word 'rake' mentioned by several.

Genevieve kept her gaze forward, refusing to shrink under the scrutiny of the Ton. For the first time, their censure held no power over her. She had chosen to follow her heart, and she would face the consequences without regret.

Sebastian leaned closer; his breath warm against her ear. "Pay them no mind. This night belongs to us alone."

A blush stained her cheeks at his intimate tone and possessive claim, though she could not deny the thrill it evoked. She struggled against the dictates of society and her own doubts and fears. But in this moment, she felt profoundly free. She glanced up at Sebastian, at the man she had chosen, and smiled. "So it shall be, my lord."

Arm in arm, they took to the ballroom floor, ready to face the whispers and stares of the Ton together. Genevieve's heart swelled with pleasure and purpose. She had made her choice at last. The ballroom was awash with colour and sound. Ladies in jewel-toned gowns of emerald, ruby and sapphire satin swished across the dance floor, their partners clad in formal black tailcoats. A lively orchestra played a spirited tune as couples danced, conversed and promenaded around the perimeter of the room.

Sebastian guided Genevieve onto the dance and drew her into his arms. As they began the steps of the quadrille, she marvelled at how perfectly they moved together, as if they had danced this way for years.

"Have I told you how ravishing you look tonight?" Sebastian murmured, his gaze smouldering as it swept over her.

Heat rose in Genevieve's cheeks. "You have not, but I shall not object if you feel inclined to compliment me further."

His lips curved into a teasing smile. "Minx. You know precisely how to capture my interest, don't you?"

"I haven't the faintest idea what you mean," she replied archly.

"Little liar," he laughed, pulling her closer as the steps of the dance brought them together. "You have captured far more than my interest, Genevieve, and you know it."

Her breath caught at the sincerity in his tone. The rumours and whispers of Sebastian's reputation faded into the background, overshadowed by the truth she saw in his eyes. However unwise it may be, her heart was irrevocably his. She squeezed his hand gently in response, and they continued their dance in comfortable silence, simply enjoying each other's company.

After dancing with Sebastian, Genevieve excused herself to grab a glass of lemonade. Sebastian was pulled away into conversation with several of his parliamentary companions. Lady Penelope bustled over to the refreshment table. "Genevieve! There you are. You have made rather an impression on one young gentleman." Genevieve blushed. "He has just asked for your hand in marriage!" Genevieve glanced to where Sebastian was still conversing with his friends. Her brow furrowed. "Lord Avery has been so enamoured with you he could not wait till morning to ask."

"Lord Avery? Mama, are you sure he asked for me? I have not spoken more than a few words to the man since our return. Could it be possible that he meant Georgina?"

"Do not be silly dear, of course he meant you. He even commented on your dress tonight." Lady Penelope regarded her daughter with a curious gaze.

"Mama, I do not accept! I do not wish to marry Lord Avery!" Genevieve looked for Sebastian for help, however, he appeared to have disappeared into the crowed. Panic swelled within her.

"You will accept. Your father has already agreed. Lord Avery is the perfect match. We will have no more discussion. If you cannot agree to this, we will leave this instant. I know I said you should follow your heart, but I did not think you would seriously contemplate Mordesley."

"Mother! I cannot…" Genevieve's arm was pulled harshly by her mother. Her mother stopped a footman to leave word for her father and Georgina that they had left early and would send the carriage back for them.

Genevieve was pulled from the ballroom, all the while straining to see if she could see Sebastian in the sea of people.

Chapter Seven

Sebastian stared moodily into the crackling fire, absently swirling brandy in his glass. The laughter and boisterous chatter of his companions at the club faded into the background as his thoughts turned, inevitably, to Genevieve.

Ever since seeing her at his ball, he had been unable to get her out of his mind. The talk of her marrying Lord Avery was the talk of White's, and had sparked an unexpectedly fierce surge of jealousy. He knew he had no claim over her, not after the way he had hurt her in their youth. But the look in her eyes when they danced, as though she had found her heart's desire...it haunted him.

A rough clap on the back jolted him from his reverie. Lord Aynslie dropped onto the leather sofa beside him, cheeks ruddy from drink. "Come now, Mordesley, you've been brooding all evening. Out with it. What has you in such a state?"

Sebastian forced a casual shrug. "Nothing of import. Just weary, I suppose."

"Poppycock. I know that look." Aynslie leaned closer, reeking of brandy and stale cigars. "This is about a woman, eh? Got your eye on some fetching lass your friends don't know about?"

Sebastian tensed. Aynslie may be a fool, but he was uncomfortably perceptive at times. "As if I have time for such dalliances these days," he said lightly. "My schedule allows little opportunity for female companionship."

"Ha! Never stopped you before." Aynslie prodded his arm. "Come now, we're your bosom companions, aren't we? You can tell us."

With a muttered oath, Sebastian stood, the need to escape suddenly overwhelming. "Excuse me, gentlemen. I find I am out of sorts this evening."

Before they could protest, he strode from the room, dropping his glass onto a footman's tray with a careless clatter. The din of the club faded blessedly behind him as he escaped into the night.

The cold air helped clear his head, though it did little to ease the restless energy thrumming through his veins. He had to see her. Had to know if the connection he'd felt between them, however brief, had only been a figment of his imagination.

Hailing a hackney, he gave the driver directions to the St. Claire townhouse. Reckless, perhaps, calling at such a late hour, but he was past caring about propriety. He had to know if the glimpse he'd caught of the vibrant, clever woman beneath her polished exterior had been real. And if, by some miracle, she might still care for him too.

The carriage rolled to a stop before the stately townhouse. Sebastian paid the driver and straightened his coat, steeling his nerves. Before he could lose his resolve, he strode up the steps and rapped the ornate knocker.

After a moment, the door creaked open. The butler's eyes widened in surprise at the sight of him. "Lord Mordesley. How may I be of service?"

"I apologise for the late hour, but I must speak with Lady Genevieve at once. It is a matter of urgency."

The butler hesitated. "I regret Lady Genevieve has retired for the evening. Perhaps you could call again tomorrow…"

"Please." Sebastian pitched his voice low. "I would not ask if it were not important."

After a brief internal struggle, the butler nodded reluctantly and stepped aside. "Wait here. I shall inquire if she is able to receive you."

Sebastian released a breath as the door clicked shut. Reckless indeed, and very improper, but he was committed now. He could only hope Genevieve would consent to see him so late unchaperoned.

At last, footsteps sounded, and the door swung open once more. Genevieve stood haloed in candlelight, surprise and wariness etched on her delicate features. She was clad only in a dressing gown, her hair falling in chestnut waves about her shoulders. Sebastian's pulse quickened at the sight.

"My lord," she said uncertainly. "To what do I owe the honour?"

Sebastian removed his hat, suddenly feeling like a wayward schoolboy called to task. "Forgive the intrusion, Lady Genevieve. I know it is quite improper but...I had to speak with you."

She studied him a moment, then stepped aside in tacit permission to enter. The butler hovered anxiously as Sebastian crossed the threshold into the marble-tiled foyer.

"You may leave us," Genevieve said. The butler looked askance but dared not argue with a lady of the house. With a bow, he took his leave, leaving the door open to the servant area.

Alone with Genevieve, the words seemed to stick in Sebastian's throat. She gazed at him expectantly, one delicate brow raised. He cleared his throat, cursing himself for a fool.

"There are rumours you plan to accept Lord Avery's proposal," he finally managed.

Genevieve blinked. "If I did, that is hardly your concern."

Sebastian winced at her cool tone. "You're right, of course. It's only that I..." He raked a hand through his hair in frustration. "Forgive me, I don't know what I hoped to achieve by coming here. Only that when I heard the news, I felt I had to see you. Had to know if..."

He broke off as Genevieve's eyes softened. "Oh, Sebastian," she sighed. "I told you; the past is behind us now. It's best we both accept that."

His chest constricted at her words. She was slipping through his fingers and the thought filled him with desperation. "Don't marry him," he blurted out.

Genevieve stiffened. "I beg your pardon?"

"Avery. He's not right for you." Sebastian took an impulsive step closer. "We both know that."

"You know nothing of what is right for me," Genevieve said sharply. "Not anymore."

The rebuke stung, but Sebastian refused to relent just yet. "I know he cannot make you happy. Not truly. He is dull as a post, and you, my dear, are far too clever for the likes of him." A hint of a smile teased his lips. "You'd eat him alive."

Genevieve's lips twitched before she mastered herself. "You forget yourself, sir. My arrangements are none of your affair." She brushed past him toward the stairs. "I think it's best you take your leave."

Panic lanced through him as she began climbing the steps, candlelight flickering over her silhouette. He could not just let her slip away, not like this.

"Don't do it," he entreated, hating the desperation in his voice. "Don't choose duty over love. You'll regret it."

Genevieve paused, one hand resting on the banister. Sebastian held his breath, praying she would relent. After an agonising moment, she glanced back, eyes glinting in the shadows.

"The heart doesn't rule everything, no matter what the poets say." Her words held an air of finality that crushed his flimsy hopes. "Good night, my lord."

She disappeared down the corridor, leaving Sebastian staring after her, bereft. She had made her choice, and it was not him. The pain of rejection was even more acute than he had anticipated.

With a heavy heart, he took his leave, Genevieve's parting words echoing in his mind. Perhaps she was right, and it was time he accept that their paths were meant to diverge rather than entwine. She deserved happiness, even if it was not with him. He only prayed she would not come to regret the choice she had made this night.

As his carriage ambled through the near-empty streets, melancholy weighed heavily on Sebastian's shoulders. He should be focused on his political career and familial duties, not pining after past infatuations. And yet…

He thought back on their youthful friendship, before passions and tempers had intervened. Genevieve's clever wit, her thirst for adventure, the way her eyes would light with exhilaration whenever they stole away on another escapade. He had loved her, he realised now. Not with the heated impulsiveness of first love perhaps, but with a deep and abiding affection.

She had been a steady confidante throughout his turbulent adolescence when the rest of his world seemed upside down.

Until he had ruined everything with his thoughtless selfishness.

Sebastian sighed, rubbing his temples wearily. No use dwelling on past mistakes. Genevieve had made her choice, and he would not disrespect her by pursuing her further. A clean break was best for them both.

Yet even as he told himself this, he knew that losing Genevieve would leave a hollow ache inside him no amount of revelry or political success could fill. She had sparked something in him, awakened feelings and dreams he'd thought long buried. To give her up now seemed akin to relinquishing his heart.

The next day, Sebastian arrived at White's half-heartedly hoping word from Genevieve awaited him. Perhaps she had changed her mind and reconsidered his proposal. But he found no note awaiting him. News of her betrothal to Avery, however, reached his ears soon enough.

His companions ribbed him on his subdued mood, amused to see the usually carefree marquess so out of sorts. Sebastian put on a brave face, joining in their banter and forcing the occasional laugh. Inside, however, the news of Genevieve's engagement sat like a stone in the pit of his stomach.

"Bad luck, old chap," Aynslie consoled with a smack on his back. "Never fun to lose a pretty bird to some other fellow. But plenty more lovely ladies await your charms, eh? No use dwelling on this one."

Sebastian managed a thin smile. If only it were so simple to forget her. But he had lost more than a potential dalliance or conquest. He had lost his chance to reclaim the easy affection and mutual understanding they had once shared, before youthful mistakes had driven them apart.

Their estrangement had left an ache inside Sebastian, an empty space where she had once occupied. He saw that now. And the realisation that the rift between them could never be repaired cut deeper than any lost romance.

Over the next few days, Sebastian threw himself into his political duties and social engagements, desperate for distraction. He attended parliamentary sessions, dined with powerful connections, and laughed uproariously at the theatre as if his heart wasn't quietly breaking.

But his smiles never reached his eyes, and his laughter held an edge of manic desperation. In unguarded moments, his thoughts strayed constantly to Genevieve, reopening the wound over and over.

He had lost her. Truly lost her this time. She would never again turn to him with that spark of mischief in her eyes, tempting him to join in some reckless adventure against his better judgment. He could not make her laugh with silly jokes or listen patiently as she confided her innermost dreams.

That easy, profound connection between them was gone, severed by the foolish impetuousness of his youth and the five years apart. And the weight of what could have been, what should have been, threatened to crush him beneath waves of remorse and regret.

So, Sebastian continued his relentless quest for distraction. If he kept moving, kept laughing and charming his way through London's soirees, perhaps he could outrun the emptiness dogging his steps. For a time, he could forget the hollow ache of loneliness, and pretend the life he was living was enough.

Chapter Eight

Several weeks later…

The morning sun filtered through lace curtains, dappling Genevieve's hands as she clasped them in her lap. She sat motionless on the settee, her gaze fixed unseeing on the Persian rug unfurled before her.

Try as she might, she could not banish the Marquess of Mordesley from her thoughts. His piercing grey eyes, the curve of his lips as he regarded her over the rim of a champagne flute, the timbre of his voice as he leaned close to whisper some witty remark.

Genevieve sighed and turned her head to gaze out the window, where a breeze rustled the leaves of the chestnut trees. She knew she should not think of Sebastian Mordesley so, and yet her traitorous mind insisted on recalling every detail of their encounters.

Though she tried to remind herself of his rakish reputation. She could not ignore the way her heart quickened at the sight of him or the thrill of anticipation she felt each time she entered a ballroom in hopes he would be there. She had decided to give her heart to Sebastian, but that did not mean she should marry the man.

"Really, Genevieve, you must stop this foolishness at once." She straightened and clasped her hands tighter, summoning her resolve. She would not throw away her reputation and future on a whim. There were more suitable gentlemen who could make her a proper husband, like Lord Avery.

Still, she could not banish Sebastian from her thoughts, no matter how she tried. Each time she told herself it was impossible, her mind conjured the memory of his gaze meeting hers across a crowded room, and a traitorous warmth blossomed inside her.

She rose abruptly and paced to the window, pressing a hand to her chest. She knew following her heart would only lead to ruin, and yet she could not ignore its pleas. How she wished she had been born a man, free to live as she chose instead of forever struggling against the constraints of propriety.

Genevieve closed her eyes, listening to the rustle of leaves outside. She was no closer to conquering her feelings for the Marquess, but she steeled herself anew. She would do as duty demanded, even if it meant locking away her heart forever.

Genevieve descended the stairs to join her mother for tea, smoothing the skirts of her plum muslin gown. She had chosen a simple but elegant style, as befitted an unmarried lady of quality entertaining a suitor.

Lord Avery stood as she entered the drawing room, bowing over her hand. "My dear Lady Genevieve, you look delightful as always."

"Your lordship is too kind." She managed a wan smile and took a seat across from him. Though he was handsome and charming, she could not stir any real affection for him in her breast. Not when her heart already belonged to another.

"I have been anticipating this visit all week," he said, leaning forward eagerly. "I missed your company at Almack's on Tuesday for their recital day."

"My apologies." The platitude sounded hollow on her lips. How she envied the freedom of men to live as they chose, unbound by the expectations of marriage and family. Yet she had a duty to her parents and station to make a suitable match, no matter her own desires.

Lord Avery prattled on about the latest on-dits and his new phaeton, but Genevieve scarcely heard him. Her gaze drifted to the window, where sunlight filtered through the curtains. Somewhere out in London, Sebastian was going about his day, as carefree and unfettered as always. She wondered if he ever spared a thought for the woman who could not stop thinking of him.

With an effort, she turned her attention back to Lord Avery. This was her fate now, to entertain insipid men and feign interest in idle chatter. She swallowed the lump in her throat and summoned a smile, embracing the shackles of propriety once more.

Lord Avery paused, eyeing her with concern. "You seem distracted today, Lady Genevieve. Is something amiss?"

"Not at all," she lied. "My thoughts wandered for a moment, but I am quite focused on your company now."

His brow remained furrowed, unsatisfied. "If there is anything troubling you, I hope you will share it with me. As your suitor, your happiness and well-being are of the utmost importance to me."

His words, though well-meaning, only underscored the vast differences between Lord Avery and Sebastian. The marquess had always seen through her pretences, able to sense her moods and thoughts with an almost uncanny ability. Lord Avery, for all his courtesy, barely scratched the surface.

She gave him another smile, this one tinged with sadness. "You are too kind. But there is nothing to trouble you with, my lord, truly."

He took her hand, his grip overly warm and damp. "I hope that we continue to grow closer, so you will feel comfortable confiding in me as a devoted husband."

Husband. The word sent a ripple of panic through her. She had walked eyes open into this courtship, willing to sacrifice her heart's desire for duty and propriety. But now the reality of it loomed before her, a future as bleak and stifling as a prison cell.

She stared at their joined hands, a vice slowly squeezing the breath from her lungs. All her resolve wavered and crumbled, destroyed by a single word. In that moment, she knew with stark and sudden clarity that she could not marry Lord Avery. Not when her heart would always belong to Sebastian.

Genevieve withdrew her hand from Lord Avery's grip, the warmth of his touch now unpleasant. She clasped her hands before her, struggling to maintain a neutral expression.

"Forgive me, my lord, I am not quite myself today." The excuse sounded weak even to her own ears, but she could think of nothing else.

He frowned, brows drawing together. "Are you unwell? Should I call for your maid?"

"No, no. Just a headache, I assure you." She forced another smile. "It will pass."

"Then I shall not tax you further." He bowed, the picture of a concerned suitor. "May I call on you again this week?"

She opened her mouth, the refusal perched on the tip of her tongue. But she swallowed it back, nodding instead. "That would be lovely."

After he took his leave, she stood for a long moment in the parlour, listening to the echo of the closing door. Her heart felt torn to ribbons, pulled in too many directions at once. She yearned to flee from these gilded walls that seemed to close in around her, trapping her in a life not of her choosing.

A life without Sebastian.

The thought brought tears to her eyes, a sob rising in her throat. She pressed the back of her hand to her mouth, staunching the sound before it could escape. She knew now, with a certainty that could not be denied, that she could not continue the courtship with Lord Avery. The consequences would be dire, the scandal enough to shake the very foundations of the ton. But she would face it all, and gladly, if it meant she could be with the man she loved.

The only question that remained was whether Sebastian felt the same. Whether he would defy society expectations and risk everything for her, as she would for him. Her heart swelled with hope, a smile curving her lips. If anyone was daring enough to throw propriety to the wind and follow where his heart led, it was the marquess. She had only to tell him the truth, and together they would face whatever may come.

The next morning, Genevieve sat stiffly beside Lord Avery in his carriage as they made their way to Hyde Park for a promenade. Though the sun shone brightly outside, she felt enveloped in gloom. Every smile she forced felt false, every word that passed between them hollow. She needed to be sure of Sebastian's feelings before rejecting Lord Avery, lest his feelings be different from hers.

How had she deluded herself into thinking this courtship could lead to happiness? Lord Avery was amiable and respectable, but there was no spark of passion or meeting of minds. No matter how she tried, she could not feel for him what she felt for Sebastian.

As the carriage rolled through the gates of the park, her gaze instinctively searched the crowds. *Would he be here today?* Her heart quickened at the thought, though she scolded herself for such foolishness.

"Shall we walk, my lady?" Lord Avery extended his arm. With a sigh, Genevieve took it, stepping down from the carriage to stroll the path at his side.

They had not gone far when a familiar figure strode into view, clad in riding gear astride a magnificent black stallion. Genevieve's breath caught in her throat at the sight of Sebastian, her steps slowing as her eyes drank in every detail. He had not yet noticed them in the crowd, his gaze scanning the promenade. She willed him to look her way, fighting the urge to call out and wave him down.

"Is something amiss?" Lord Avery asked, frowning at her distraction.

Genevieve started, colour rising in her cheeks. "Forgive me," she murmured. "I thought I saw an acquaintance in the crowd." Before he could question her further, a mother's shriek rang out as a child followed a ball rolling into the path of oncoming horses. In an instant, chaos erupted around them. Genevieve bit back a cry.

Sebastian spurred his stallion into action, deftly swooping down to snatch the ball and child both from harm's way. The crowd erupted into applause as he handed the wide-eyed boy back to his frantic mother, tipping his hat in a casual display of heroism.

Genevieve's heart swelled with pride and longing as she watched him, a wistful smile touching her lips. No matter how she tried to resist him, he always managed to win her over in the end.

"You seem quite taken with the marquess," Lord Avery observed, a hint of jealousy in his tone. "Fool child to run in front of the horses like that, one of them may have been injured. Mordesley may have injured his own horse wheeling him round like that to grab the child."

She shook her head, forcing her gaze away from Sebastian. "His actions were admirable, but I have no particular affection for the man himself."

"Come now, there's no need to be coy." He frowned down at her, suspicion etched into his features. "Rumour has it the two of you were once quite close. Is there any truth to that?"

Panic rose in Genevieve's chest as she struggled to compose a convincing denial. But before she could respond, a familiar voice spoke behind them.

"Lady Genevieve, Lord Avery. What a pleasant surprise."

Sebastian. Her heart fluttered at the sound of his voice, though she kept her expression neutral upon turning to face him. "My Lord," she greeted with a polite curtsy.

"I was just inquiring about the nature of your relationship with the lady," Lord Avery said, a hint of challenge in his tone as he eyed Sebastian.

Sebastian's gaze flickered briefly to Genevieve, a ghost of a smile playing at his lips. "The lady and I have been friends for some years." His eyes held a glimmer of knowing amusement. "Though I'm afraid the particulars of our relationship are private."

Heat rose in Genevieve's cheeks at the implication in his words. This encounter could not end soon enough.

Lord Avery frowned, clearly displeased by Sebastian's evasive response. "I see. Then you won't mind it when I pay Lady Genevieve a call this afternoon."

It was a bold challenge, meant to assert his claim of betrothed in the face of Sebastian's ambiguous remarks. Genevieve opened her mouth to object, but Sebastian spoke first.

"That won't be possible, I'm afraid. Lady Genevieve has already accepted an invitation to accompany me on a ride through Hyde Park."

Shock rendered Genevieve momentarily speechless. She had done no such thing.

Lord Avery's eyes narrowed. "Has she indeed?" He looked to Genevieve for confirmation, his expression clouded with suspicion.

Panic and dismay warred within her as all eyes turned to await her response. To side with Sebastian would only add fuel to rumours of an improper relationship. But to deny his claim might provoke him into revealing details about their past that she was not prepared to acknowledge in front of Lord

Avery.

She faltered, grasping for words that might extricate her from this undesirable situation without damage to her reputation. But before she found them, Lord Avery made a contemptuous sound.

"It seems I have been misled as to your character, Lady Genevieve. I bid you good day." With a curt bow, he turned on his heel and strode away.

Genevieve watched him go, equal parts indignant and relieved. A broken betrothal would cause ruin, scandal and the possibility of never marrying, but, Avery's jealousy showed a side to him that was less than desirable. As soon as his form disappeared into the crowd, she rounded on Sebastian.

"How dare you!" Anger coloured her hushed exclamation. "What possible reason could you have for embarrassing me in such a way? Do you realise the damage you have caused?"

"My apologies," he said, though his expression held more amusement than contrition. "I couldn't resist intervening when I saw that odious man bothering you."

"You had no right," she insisted. "My associations are no concern of yours."

"Come now, Genevieve." His voice softened as he regarded her, a familiar warmth seeping into his gaze. "Must we continue these petty pretences? There was a time when my concern for your well-being and happiness was not so easily dismissed. I feel an obligation to you, like a sister."

A blush crept into her cheeks as she glanced away, discomfited by the affection in his eyes. The memory of simpler days when she might have welcomed such concern still lingered, but the word sister stuck in her mind. She knew then that his feelings for her were not the same as her own. "That time has passed," she said quietly, steeling herself against the ache in her chest. "We have gone our separate ways. It is best if we remain as strangers."

"If that is truly what you wish."

His concession only served to deepen her sadness. But she held fast to her conviction. To relent now would be to resurrect dreams of a future that could never be.

Summoning the last dregs of her resolve, she raised her eyes to his. "It is."

For a long moment he studied her in silence, as if searching for any remaining trace of the girl he once knew. At length, he sighed.

"Very well. I shall trouble you no further." He bowed, a look of grim acceptance on his face. "Good day, Lady Genevieve."

"Good day, my lord."

She watched him disappear into the crowd, an ache blooming within her chest. However necessary this parting might be, it did not make it any less painful. Blinking back the sting of tears, she steeled herself and moved on through the park.

Genevieve struggled to maintain her composure as she made her way back home. While she had succeeded in convincing Sebastian of the futility of rekindling their association, she had not fooled herself. The memory of their parting continued to haunt her, awakening bittersweet recollections of the past and longings she had thought buried forever. Only as she neared home did she realise she did not have a chaperone, that Mordesley had left her undefended. The rake!

Genevieve sought out her dear friend Amelia. If any could offer guidance, it was Amelia.

She found her friend in the garden, strolling along the gravel path with a book in hand. At Genevieve's approach, Amelia glanced up, her eyes widening in concern at the sight of her friend's obvious distress.

"Oh, Genevieve, what has happened? You look quite overwrought." She tucked her book under one arm and grasped Genevieve's hands in her own.

Genevieve squeezed Amelia's hands gratefully. "It is Lord Avery," she said with a heavy sigh. "We have parted ways, and not amicably. I fear I have acted hastily and shall live to regret it."

"What?" Amelia exclaimed. "But you seemed so well-matched. Has there been a falling out?"

"Not in the usual sense." Genevieve shook her head, a wry smile twisting her lips. "You see, I could not go through with it. However suitable the match might have appeared to others, I found I had no true affection for the man. When it came time to pledge my heart, I realised it was not mine to give. Yet I then spoke with the man that does own it and the words like a sister came from his mouth."

"Oh, Genevieve." Amelia's expression softened with understanding. "You did not love Avery."

"No," Genevieve admitted. "I do not. I thought perhaps affection might grow in time, but I cannot build a marriage on false pretences. It would be a slow ruin for us both."

"You have done the right thing," Amelia said firmly. "A loveless marriage is a tragedy. You deserve so much more than that."

Genevieve smiled gratefully at her friend. "I had hoped you might say as much. Yet now my reputation is at stake, and my mother will be furious. I fear the path ahead shall not be easy."

"Let them gossip," Amelia said with a dismissive wave of her hand. "In the end, you must follow your heart. True happiness cannot be found by conforming to the expectations of others."

Heart lightening, Genevieve squeezed her friend's hands once more. "Thank you. I needed to hear that. Though I notice you do not seem to overwhelmed with suitors."

Amelia smiled. "That is what friends are for. Not everyone wishes to marry, I am waiting father out so when I am of age I can become a governess. Now, tell me what comes next in this grand adventure of yours!"

Though her friend's words resonated deeply, Genevieve could not dismiss her worries so easily. Society judged harshly those who dared step outside its strict boundaries, and as a woman of noble birth, she was under constant scrutiny. If she chose to follow her heart's desire rather than her duty, it would reflect poorly not only on herself but also on her family. Her mother in particular would see it as a personal failing.

These thoughts chased themselves in endless circles through Genevieve's mind as Amelia's borrowed carriage rolled through the streets of London. By the time she arrived home, tension had knotted in her stomach. She dreaded facing her mother, whose sharp gaze would no doubt discern that something was amiss.

When the footman opened the carriage door, Genevieve steeled herself and stepped down with as much poise as she could muster. As always, her mother stood in the foyer to greet her, peering at Genevieve over the rim of her spectacles.

"You are late returning," she said coolly. "Lord Avery was quite put out at your absence from this afternoon's engagement."

Genevieve lowered her eyes, heart pounding. "Forgive me, Mother. I stopped to call on Amelia and lost track of the hour. Though I thought Lord Avery might not come given our disagreement this morning."

"Hmph. See that it does not happen again. I still do not know why he insisted in taking you out this morning, it was not the correct hour." Her mother's gaze sharpened. "Is something the matter? You seem distressed."

Summoning all her courage, Genevieve looked up to meet that piercing stare. "Mother, there is something we must discuss."

Her mother's eyebrows rose a fraction. "Indeed? This sounds serious. Come, we shall take tea in the drawing room."

Genevieve's courage nearly deserted her as she entered the parlour where her mother sat pouring tea. The weight of the conversation to come felt like stones pressing upon her chest. She perched on the edge of a floral brocade chair across from her mother, folding her hands tightly in her lap.

"You wished to speak with me?" Her mother peered at her over the rim of the teacup, eyes narrowed.

Genevieve opened her mouth, but no words emerged. She pressed her lips together and swallowed hard, willing her voice not to shake.

"Well?" Impatience edged her mother's tone. "I don't have all day, Genevieve."

Drawing a quavering breath, Genevieve forced herself to meet her mother's expectant gaze. "I cannot marry Lord Avery."

Her mother froze, teacup halfway to her lips. "I beg your pardon?"

"My heart lies elsewhere." Genevieve gripped the folds of her gown, the rustle of fabric thunderous in the heavy silence.

Her mother's teacup clattered against the saucer. "With whom?" she demanded, eyes flashing. "Tell me this instant, girl."

Genevieve lifted her chin. "The Marquess of Mordesley. I love him, Mama."

Her mother surged to her feet. "Have you lost your senses?" she thundered. "The marquess is entirely unsuitable. You will end this foolishness at once and accept Lord Avery. He is the match I have chosen. I allowed your foolishness with Mordesley at the beginning as I thought his reputation would eventually get to you. You will marry Lord Avery, everything has been set."

"I cannot. I do not love him." Genevieve's voice trembled but she held firm even as her mother's face purpled with rage.

"Ungrateful wretch! After all I have done to secure your future." Spittle flew from her lips. "Very well. If you insist on ruining yourself, you will receive not one penny of support from me."

It was the ultimatum Genevieve had dreaded, yet the quiet determination in her mother's tone cut far deeper than shouting ever could.

"Mama, please..." she whispered, the rejection piercing her heart like an icy dagger.

Her mother's eyes were hard and flinty. "My decision is final. Now remove yourself from my sight."

Blinking back a burning sting of tears, Genevieve rose on trembling legs. She turned her back on the woman who had nurtured her, shaped her, yet would now cast her out without a second thought. Her slippered feet whispered across the oriental rug, the agonised pounding of her heart drowning out all other sounds.

This was the price of following her heart, but she could pay it no other way. She had chosen her path, and now she must walk it alone. But she would walk it proudly, with her head held high. Her heart swelled at the thought of Sebastian, who seemed to love her in return, propriety be damned. Together, they would forge their own path.

Come what may, she would not falter. Love was worth any price.

Genevieve wandered the gardens of her family estate, her mind churning with turbulent emotions. Though she had made her choice with conviction, doubt still lingered. She loved Sebastian with all her heart, but was love enough? They would face hardships, disapproval, and scandal for their unexpected match. Could their love withstand the trials to come?

A familiar voice interrupted her brooding reverie. "My darling, what troubles you?"

She turned to find her father sitting on a bench. "Mother has disowned me

60

for refusing Lord Avery's suit. I told her I was in love with Lord Mordesley and that I wished to pursue that match."

"Ah. Except your mother does not decide that. You will always have a home here sweetheart. We did not disown your brother when he was seen duelling. We are not going to disown you for loving someone. Plus, I have a secret. Someone has just arrived from Rome. He will be here for dinner."

"Gregory? Business in Rome has wrapped up?" Genevieve laughed and threw herself forward to embrace her father.

Chapter Nine

Sebastian strode through Hyde Park, gravel crunching beneath his boots as he sought solitude from the inane chatter and posturing that seemed to permeate London's social scene. The sun was warm on his face, a light breeze rustling the leaves overhead, yet inner turmoil roiled within him.

Ever since catching a glimpse of Lady Genevieve St. Claire at the Henry's ball last week, he had been unable to banish her from his thoughts. The spark of defiance in her eyes when they'd locked gazes across the ballroom had stirred something in him, an intrigue he thought long dormant.

Try as he might, Sebastian could not help imagining crossing paths with her again, peering beneath the veil of polite indifference to connecting with the woman she had become. But such contemplations were foolish, and dangerous. Nothing good could come of renewing his acquaintance with Genevieve St. Claire. Their history was fraught enough without adding further entanglements to the mix.

Lost in thought, Sebastian did not notice the approaching figure until she spoke, jolting him from his reverie.

"Fancy seeing you here, Lord Mordesley."

He turned to find Lady Constance beaming up at him, a vision in violet silk. As always, a shiver of distaste rippled through him at her lavish display of charm. They had ended their dalliance months ago at his insistence, yet she continued hounding him at every turn. Sebastian forced a smile.

"Lady Constance. A pleasure, as always."

She drifted closer, laying a hand on his arm. "Come now, must you be so formal? I feel we know each other better than that."

Sebastian tensed, gently extracting his arm from her grip. "Forgive me, I did not mean to give offense. But I am expected at White's shortly and should be on my way."

A pretty pout crossed her rosebud lips. "Must you rush off so soon? I had hoped we could talk privately. I've missed our little…chats."

His jaw clenched at her insinuation, but he kept his tone light. "Perhaps another time. Please excuse me."

With a perfunctory bow, he turned and strode off down the path before she could protest further. Constance had always been possessive, but her behaviour was growing increasingly brazen. He would have to take more care to avoid her, or risk further damage to his reputation.

Though in truth, Sebastian mused, his reputation was already beyond salvaging. His exploits had earned him a certain notoriety, one he could neither escape nor take pride in. Not when the careless dalliances of his youth had brought such pain to the one woman who had once truly mattered.

The familiar ache of regret pulled at his chest. No matter how he tried to move beyond the past, it clung to him like a spectre, reminding him of the man he might have been had arrogance not blinded him. Perhaps it was no less than he deserved, to walk through life shadowed by remorse.

Lost in melancholy thoughts, Sebastian did not immediately notice the approaching figure until a cough drew his attention. He glanced up to find an auburn-haired gentleman staring with unconcealed rancour, Gregory St. Claire.

"Lord Ashford," Sebastian growled. The impetuous St. Claire heir who had nearly cost them both their lives in a reckless duel. Another ghost come back to haunt him.

Gregory's lip curled in contempt. "Mordesley. I might have known you'd be skulking about, looking to ensnare another innocent girl."

"You go too far, sir," Sebastian bit out. "I've as much right to be here as you."

"Debatable. Our duel was not finished, only you managed to get away before anyone saw." Gregory shifted. "Now state your business or be on your way."

Humiliating as it was to be driven off like a vagabond, Sebastian recognised the futility of prolonged confrontation. With a terse nod, he turned abruptly and continued on his way, Gregory's glare boring into his back. The encounter left an ashen taste in his mouth that had naught to do with the other man's accusations.

Some wounds even time could not mend.

By the time Sebastian arrived home, robes of melancholy had fully descended upon him. He waved off his butler and made straight for his study, hoping solitude and a glass of brandy might dispel the cloud that clung to his spirit.

But as he stared into the fire's dying embers, no amount of spirits could dull the ache. For the first time in forever, the prospect of a life unmarked by Genevieve's presence seemed unbearably bleak. A chance encounter in the park had reawakened memories and longings he thought long buried.

With a muffled curse, Sebastian downed the remnants of his glass. Such maudlin ponderings accomplished nothing. Genevieve St. Claire belonged to his past, and there she must remain if he hoped to have any future worth living.

Still, some traitorous part of his heart whispered that a life lived without love might be the bleakest future of all.

A knock interrupted his brooding, and his butler entered upon being bid enter. "Pardon the intrusion, my lord, but Viscount Gregory Ashford is here requesting an audience. Shall I show him in?"

Sebastian straightened, surprise piercing through his malaise. Gregory St. Claire, here? After that afternoon's encounter Sebastian had thought, the man would want to avoid him at all costs. So, what was he here now?

"Send him in," Sebastian said, curiosity somewhat outweighing his wariness.

A moment later, Lord Ashford prowled into the study, auburn hair glinting red gold in the sunlight. He looked travel-worn, his clothes finely made but rumpled. "Mordesley," he greeted neutrally.

Sebastian inclined his head. "Ashford. This is an unexpected surprise."

One shoulder lifted in a shrug. "I came back to face my demons, I suppose." His gaze sharpened. "And make amends where necessary. This afternoon in the park you surprised me, I acted in a manner unbecoming of me."

Sebastian stilled, instincts prickling. But Gregory's expression held no hostility or judgment. Only weariness, and perhaps regret. "The past is behind us," Sebastian said carefully.

"Is it?" Gregory stared at him for a long moment. Then his taut shoulders slumped, resignation replacing wariness. "I behaved rashly back then. Nearly killed you in a fool's quest for honour." His lips twisted. "We all made mistakes. Genevieve most of all. But I should not have challenged you as I did. It was unworthy of us both."

Sebastian blinked, rendered momentarily speechless. "It is I who need to apologise. These last few weeks I have come to see the amazing woman your sister has become. I should not have done as I did before you left. You called me out on my behaviour, yet it was you who paid the price. I hope you and I can become friends."

"No Mordesley. I don't think we will ever be friends. I have heard that my sister has broken Lord Avery's engagement. If I find you had anything to do with it, I will find a more discrete way to bring you down than a duel." Gregory dipped his head in farewell and left Sebastian sitting confused and a little bit hopeful. Genevieve had broken her engagement? Had that incident in the park truly have cause a break? If it had, Lord Avery was more of a fool than Sebastian had taken him for.

Chapter Ten

The morning sun filtered through the curtains of Lord Gregory's study as Genevieve settled into one of the worn leather armchairs by the fireplace. Her brother gazed at her with patient concern, his weathered features creased into a frown.

Genevieve clasped her hands in her lap, gathering her thoughts before speaking. "I find myself in a quandary regarding Lord Mordesley."

Lord Gregory raised a brow but remained silent, waiting for her to continue. She took a deep breath, trying to quell the flutter of nerves in her stomach.

"There are moments when I believe he is not the rake Society makes him out to be. Beneath the charming facade, I glimpse a depth of character and intellect that fascinates me." She paused, watching the crackling flames. "Yet I cannot ignore the rumours surrounding his past, or the expectations placed upon my own future. A match with him would invite only scandal and censure."

Her brother leaned forward, expression softening. "My dear sister, you have always been too quick to judge based on appearances and the idle gossip of others." His eyes glinted with wisdom born of experience. "A person's character is seldom as simple as it seems. There are layers beneath layers, shaped by forces not immediately visible to an outside observer. Though need I remind you, the sixteen-year-old you thought he loved you too and look how that turned out."

Genevieve frowned, considering his words. While she had always valued propriety and duty, Lord Gregory understood the complexities of human nature. Perhaps there was more to Sebastian Mordesley than his rakish reputation suggested. Her heart quickened at the possibility, though she tried to quell the traitorous feeling. She could not throw away everything for the sake of fleeting attraction or fanciful notions of love.

Yet as much as she attempted to silence them, her brother's insights took root in her mind. She found herself wondering what layers might lie beneath Sebastian's charming veneer, and what secrets his penetrating gaze might hold.

Try as she might, she could not ignore the seed of doubt Lord Gregory had planted. Nor could she escape the insidious hope that there might be more to the Marquess of Mordesley than meets the eye.

Lord Gregory studied her pensive expression. "You wonder if there is any truth to my words in regards Mordesley." His tone softened further. "I cannot claim to know the man well, but I have glimpsed shades of depth beneath his carefree manner. A trace of melancholy in his smile, a flicker of gravity in his eyes."

He leaned back in his chair, gaze turning inward. "There was a time when I lived only for frivolous pursuits, much as Mordesley is reputed to do. But life has a way of teaching hard lessons, and beneath the glittering surface of the ton lie hidden sorrows and secret pains."

A wistful look came over his countenance. "It was a woman who taught me the error of my ways, who saw beyond my charming facade to the man beneath. Like you, she was too quick to judge based on appearances. But she gave me a chance to prove myself, and in doing so, awakened my heart to love and purpose."

He shook his head, returning to the present. "I cannot say if Mordesley will have a similar effect on you. But I ask that you look beyond idle gossip and see him for yourself. If you find naught but sin beneath the surface, you have lost nothing. I can not say I like the man. But if you glimpse the man within, as I did..."

Gregory did not finish, but his meaning was clear. Genevieve lowered her eyes, a tumult of emotions warring inside her. She thought of her duty, her reputation, all that she risked in heeding her brother's counsel. But mingled with her apprehension was the memory of Mordesley's searching gaze, and a traitorous whisper that she might uncover hidden depths if she dared to look.

Her hands tightened in her lap as she struggled between propriety and passion. Little did she realise that the seeds of her undoing had already taken root, and try as she might, she would not escape love's thorny grasp.

Genevieve sat in pensive silence, her brother's words echoing in her mind. She knew Gregory spoke from experience, having lived through his own scandalous past. If anyone understood the complexities of human nature, and the capacity for change, it was he.

Still, she hesitated. However, compelling his arguments, she could not ignore the warnings that had followed her since childhood: beware rakes and scoundrels, lest they seduce you into ruin. Mordesley's reputation was notorious, his conquests supposedly as numerous as the stars. What hope had she of reforming such a man, when scores of women before her had failed? There was also that one day five years ago in the sun dappled hallway that had started a chain of events that had led them here.

"You seem troubled, sister. Have I given you cause for concern?" Gregory asked gently.

Genevieve shook her head. "No. You have been most kind. I am simply… uncertain. I do not doubt the sincerity of your counsel, but Mordesley's character is not so easily disregarded."

"Nor should it be," her brother agreed. "No man's character is without flaw or complication. But you must look deeper than his reputation, or you will miss the truth of him."

She raised her eyes to meet his, finding reassurance in their steady warmth. "How can I be sure of what lies beneath? I have seen little to counter the rumours thus far."

"Because you have not truly seen him," Gregory said. "Not as he is, when the guards are down, and pretence falls away. The Mordesley I glimpsed is not one to be defined by idle chatter. He is a man of intellect and hidden depths, though he takes great pains to conceal them. If you can pierce that armour, as difficult as it may prove, you will find he is not the careless rake you imagine. Remember, the twenty-one-year-old him is not the now twenty-six-year-old him, just as the sixteen-year-old you is not the now twenty one year old you. In the past he may not have acted with decorum, thy does not mean that he does not now understand."

Genevieve contemplated this, imagining what might be revealed should Mordesley's charming facade fade, even for a moment. It was a tantalising prospect, though not without risk. To look closer was to hazard her heart, and all the turmoil that might follow. But Gregory had never led her astray. Perhaps it was worth the gamble, to see the truth of the man behind the myth.

She drew a steadying breath and met her brother's patient gaze. "Very well. I will look deeper, as you ask. But I make no promises beyond that."

Gregory smiled, squeezing her hands. "That is all I ask. Now, tell me of the arrangements for the ball mother has planned. I would hear more of this new musician you mean to debut."

"You mean the ball I am no longer allowed to attend as I have been disowned by mother?" Genevieve quirked an eyebrow.

The conversation turned to lighter matters, but Genevieve's thoughts remained tangled with uncertainty and possibility. Little did she know that her fate was sealed, the moment she resolved to glimpse the man beneath the rake.

That night, Genevieve lay awake in her bedchamber, moonlight filtering through velvet drapes. Her mind wandered the glittering ballrooms and dimly lit gardens she had walked with Mordesley, searching for clues she may have missed.

There were moments that gave her pause, like the wistful tone he adopted when speaking of his estate in the country, or the fleeting sorrow that shadowed his eyes when talk turned to family. He played the rake with such conviction, yet there were cracks in his armour, as Gregory said. Glimpses of something deeper, hidden beneath charm and careless mirth.

She thought of the violin in his manor, the only sign of life in those lavish rooms. He had mentioned once, in an unguarded moment, that he found solace in music. That it stirred memories of happier times, now lost to him. What sort of memories might move a man like Mordesley to melancholy? And what had caused such a light-hearted soul to seek solace at all?

There were layers to him, each one revealing something new. She had only peeled back the first, but already, she sensed the man within was far more complex than any knew. Her curiosity was piqued, despite the warnings that echoed in her mind.

Gregory was right. There was purpose to Mordesley's revelry, a reason he hid behind jests and charm. She was determined now to find it, though it meant facing risks and uncertainties that left her trembling. He had sparked her interest, this mysterious Mordesley, and she found she could not rest until his secrets were laid bare before her. The game was afoot, and Genevieve had never been one to quit when there were still moves left to make. She would play, and play well, until the truth was hers.

The next day, Genevieve found herself strolling through Hyde Park, as was her habit. The sun filtered through the leaves above in dappled shades of gold, the air crisp with the promise of autumn. Her mind wandered as she walked, turning over the puzzle of Sebastian Mordesley and how she might glimpse the man behind the mask.

So lost was she in thought, she nearly collided with a pair of gentlemen passing on horseback. At the last moment, she sidestepped, startled from her reverie.

"My apologies, Lady Genevieve," came a familiar baritone, laced with amusement. Her head snapped up to find Mordesley gazing down at her, eyes gleaming. "You seemed quite determined to throw yourself under the hooves of my poor horse. I would hate to see that pretty bonnet crushed."

Heat rose in her cheeks at the impropriety, though she refused to cower. "Perhaps you might pay more mind to where you are riding, my lord, rather than passing judgment on my choice of millinery."

His laugh was rich as brandy. "Touché." He tipped his hat to her. "Well met, my Lady. Will I see you at Lady Worthing's ball this evening?"

"You may, if the fates allow it." She dipped into a curtsy, hiding her smile.

The game was on.

After he rode off, she found her heart raced with an excitement she could not name. Their every encounter was a new move on the chessboard, each exchange a revelation. He was clever, she would grant him that, but she had not been named the cleverest of the sisters without cause. Before the night was through, she would have him in checkmate. The truth would be hers.

She strolled on through the park, anticipation simmering in her blood, as the sun dipped lower in the sky. The hunt was afoot.

The Worthing ball was a crush, the ballroom filled nearly to capacity. Genevieve scanned the room but did not immediately spy Sebastian amongst the dancers.

She accepted a glass of lemonade from a passing footman and found a place along one wall to observe. He would reveal himself in time; he could never resist making an entrance.

Sure enough, within a quarter hour a stir went through the room as Sebastian strode through the doors, resplendent in evening dress of cobalt blue, his hair gleaming in the candlelight.

He made a slow circuit of the room, laughing and greeting acquaintances, seemingly without aim. Yet she noticed he drew gradually nearer to her place by the wall. When at last he turned to scan the crowd, his gaze alit on her at once, a smile curving his lips.

"My Lady," he said, bowing before her. "The fates have indeed been kind."

"Lord Mordesley." She sank into a curtsy, then lifted her gaze to his, unable to suppress a smile of her own. "It seems they have."

"May I have the honour of the next dance?"

"You may not. I have already promised it to Lord Aynslie."

A flicker of annoyance crossed his face before he mastered himself. "The one after, then."

"We shall see." She took a delicate sip of her lemonade. "If you have behaved yourself this evening."

"And if I have not?" His eyes glinted with roguish delight. "Will you punish me as I deserve, or show me mercy?"

A blush crept into her cheeks at the implication. The man was incorrigible.

"If you continue in this vein, you shall have neither dance nor conversation from me this evening."

He pressed a hand to his heart. "You wound me, as always." But his tone was light, and admiration shone in his gaze. He wrote his name in her dance card. "Until later, then, my Lady Genevieve."

With a parting bow he left her there, disappearing into the swirl of dancers. Genevieve's heart pounded, as much from their verbal sparring as from the brief touch of his fingers against her gloved hand.

This man would be the death of her. But what a sweet surrender it would be.

Genevieve gazed after Sebastian's retreating figure, her pulse fluttering beneath the silk of her pale blue gown. Though she dared not admit it aloud, she found herself anticipating their next encounter with a mixture of delight and apprehension.

There was a vivacity to his conversation she had seldom found in other gentlemen. An unpredictability. He seemed to take as much pleasure in matching wits with her as in flirtation or seduction. Each exchange unveiled another layer of complexity in his character, another glimpse into the keen intelligence and dry humour lurking beneath his polished exterior.

She took a steadying breath, pressing a gloved hand to her chest. What was she doing? This man's reputation preceded him. However, stimulating she found his company, she could not forget the warnings and rumours that had circulated about his rakish past. Any dalliance with him would only lead to ruin.

And yet…she yearned for another dance, another conversation. A chance to solve the mystery of this man who had occupied her thoughts since the moment they met.

Across the ballroom, Sebastian glanced back at her, a slow smile curving his lips. As if he sensed the tumult of her thoughts. As if this were all some game to him, and she the next conquest to claim.

Heat rose in her cheeks. She stiffened her spine and looked away, heart pounding with equal parts desire and defiance.

Let him think what he would. She would not surrender so easily.

"There you are Lady Genevieve!" A group of young ladies swarmed over to her, led by Patricia Smythe. "My dear the most awful rumour is spreading about you. They say you have broken your engagement with Lord Avery! I say this to not be true, that you would not go back on your word. But his lordship is not here tonight and, well, the gossip runs foul."

"You heard correct, Lady Patricia. Lord Avery and I have parted ways. Unfortunately, it seems we were not well suited."

"Oh dear, well, best of luck." Patricia smirked as she and the other young ladies drifted away. Giggles and furtive glances floated back to where Genevieve stood. Across the dance floor she could see Georgina scowling at something another young lady was saying to her. Gregory had caused a stir when he entered, as many presumed him still in Rome. Now he leaned against a wall, displeasure written on his face. It seemed the sooner she could ascertain Sebastian's intentions, the better. When it was time for their dance, Sebastian was nowhere to be found.

Genevieve drifted through the remainder of the ball in a haze, torn between seeking Sebastian out and avoiding him altogether. Each time she caught a glimpse of his tall, dark figure moving through the crowds, a rush of warmth flooded her veins. Only to be replaced by the chill of fear and duty a moment later.

By the time she entered her family's carriage, a headache had settled behind her eyes from the strain of warring emotions. She pressed her fingertips to her temples with a sigh, barely registering the chatter of her sister and brother on either side of her.

Georgina's hand came to rest on her arm. "Dearest, are you quite well? You've been so quiet all evening."

Genevieve forced a smile. "Merely tired. The heat and noise of the ball have taken their toll."

"It was not the heat or noise that troubled you." Gregory's knowing gaze met hers in the dim interior of the carriage. "What is it you fear, Genevieve? That you will lose your heart to a charming rogue, or that you have already lost it?"

A blush stole over her cheeks at his perception. "I haven't lost my heart to anyone."

"But you are tempted to." His voice held no judgment, only gentle understanding. "I know the allure of risk and rebellion. The desire to follow one's passions, consequences be damned."

"Sebastian is not you," she said quietly. "His reputation—"

"Is not the whole of him. We are all capable of change...and redemption." Gregory took her hand, his eyes soft with meaning. "Do not deny yourself a chance at happiness for the sake of propriety. And do not doubt your own heart. If he is worthy of you, you will know. Do not listen to the idle gossipers either. I saw Lady Patricia talking to you and your reaction, do not let them get to you."

Genevieve gazed out the window at the passing streets, possibilities and fears chasing through her thoughts. Sebastian was a mystery she longed to solve. A dance along the edge of ruin that whispered of excitement and joy.

And her brother was right. If she was careful, if she was clever...perhaps she need not lose her heart to find love after all.

Genevieve stood before her mirror, fingers worrying the sapphire necklace at her throat as her maid styled her hair for the Smythe ball. Through the window, the sky was stained crimson and gold with the dying sun, a vivid reminder of the flames that had sparked within at Sebastian's touch.

A blush rose unbidden to her cheeks, and she wrestled to compose herself. She could not afford to be so affected, not here in the glittering ballrooms of the ton where every gesture was scrutinised. Not when the consequences of following her heart could destroy all she held dear.

"There now, my lady. You look a vision." Her maid's pleased pronouncement pulled Genevieve from her reverie. The woman in the mirror was polished and poised, every inch the aristocratic lady. But beneath the silks and jewels, her heartbeat with longing.

She sighed, smoothing a crease in her skirts. "Thank you, Clara. That will be all."

Alone, Genevieve regarded her reflection with a wry smile. Her family's expectations, the demands of her station, the whispers of society—all conspired to stand between her and the man who tempted her so. She knew the risks, the perils of throwing caution aside for a chance at love.

Tonight, she would see him again. And though she told herself to be careful, to guard her heart, she feared it was already too late. The die had been cast the moment his lips claimed hers five years ago. Now there was only surrender.

The ballroom glittered with candlelight and jewels, a vision of wealth and splendour. Genevieve glided through the crowd on her brother's arm, nodding and smiling at acquaintances while her gaze searched the room.

There. A tall, dark figure stood by one of the marble columns, a glass of brandy in one hand. His eyes locked with hers from across the floor, and a slow, knowing smile curved his lips.

"You seem distracted tonight, dear sister," Gregory said, giving her a searching look. "Is aught amiss?"

"Not at all," she said brightly. But she could feel Sebastian's gaze on her like a caress, awakening a delicious ache inside her. She dared another glance in his direction and saw something that gave her pause: a flicker of uncertainty in those cobalt eyes before his usual mask of indifference slid back into place.

It was the merest glimpse, fleeting as a shadow, but it revealed a crack in his nonchalant facade. In that moment Genevieve saw the man beneath the persona he showed the world, a man as conflicted as she was in this complicated desire that defied all reason.

The revelation stunned her. Sebastian Mordesley, the irredeemable rake, hid depths she had never suspected. There were layers to him waiting to be unravelled, a hidden self he let slip for only an instant, but which now tantalised her imagination.

Genevieve had bowed to duty and expectation. Now, she sensed the possibility of freedom, of discovering her true self as he was discovering his. The price would be scandal, estrangement from those she held dear—but as she gazed into those fathomless blue eyes, she knew she would pay it gladly. If she could but get him alone.

Genevieve smiled as she finally managed to step out onto the dancefloor with Sebastian. "Do I scare you, my lord?"

"I would not say you scare me, Lady Genevieve." He leaned closer to whisper in her ear. "Merely afraid of what you are doing to me."

"Ah, but you are a rake dear sir." Genevieve's eyes twinkled at the teasing. "Surely the thought of one little Lady is not enough to send you hiding away?"

"But the rake who has thoughts of marrying that little Lady, he, is petrified." Sebastian winked.

Genevieve's body went numb. Could he really be thinking of marrying her? It is what she wanted, but a part of her could not believe it. Their dance finished, Mordesley guided her to the side and excused himself. She was still standing in the same spot when Gregory came to collect her to go home.

The carriage rattled along the cobblestone streets, bearing Genevieve back to the townhouse she called home. But her thoughts remained with Sebastian, reliving each word and gesture that had passed between them.

When at last the carriage rolled to a stop before her family's residence, Genevieve descended with limbs grown weak from the tumult of her feelings. She bid the driver a distracted goodnight and let herself in through the front door, only to find her sister Georgina awaiting her in the foyer, she had stayed home begging off with a headache.

One look at Genevieve's expression, and Georgina's eyes narrowed shrewdly. "You've seen him again, haven't you?"

Genevieve opened her mouth, but no words emerged. What could she say that would not betray the depth of her regard for a man whose very name was anathema in respectable marriage circles?

Georgina sighed, her countenance softening with sympathy. "Oh, Genevieve. Must you insist on courting scandal and heartbreak both?"

"I know the risks," Genevieve said. "But when I'm with him, I feel alive in a way I never have before. Can you not understand why I would give anything to cling to that feeling, if only for a little while?"

"You deserve so much more than stolen moments and furtive passion." Georgina grasped her hands. "Promise me you'll be careful. Promise you won't lose your heart completely to a man who can never give you his in return."

Genevieve gazed at her sister, torn between loyalty and longing. How could she make such a promise when her heart already belonged to Sebastian, for better or for worse?

In the end, she settled for an evasion. "Do not worry. I am not so foolish as to pine for impossible things." The words tasted bitter on her tongue, but Georgina seemed satisfied.

With a sad smile, she bid Genevieve goodnight and retired to her room, leaving her alone with the memory of Sebastian's touch and the longing for so much more than she could ever have.

The next morning, Genevieve sat by the window in her bedchamber, a cup of cooling tea in her hands as she watched servants' bustle about the courtyard below. Her mind drifted to Sebastian, as it always did these days. She thought of his smile, his laughter, the warmth in his gaze when he looked at her.

Little by little, he was chipping away at her defences. She knew she should maintain a safe distance, yet she found herself powerless to resist him. Whenever they were together, the world felt brighter and more vibrant. He made her feel alive in a way she never had before.

How was she to deny herself that? To go back to the colourless existence, she had known before Sebastian re-entered her life? The prospect filled her with a bleak despair that clutched at her heart.

A knock at the door interrupted her troubled musings. "Come in," she said, hastily composing her features into a semblance of calm.

The door creaked open to reveal her friend, Lady Amelia. "Genevieve, are you quite well? You seem out of sorts this morning."

Genevieve attempted a smile, but feared it came out rather wan. "Just tired, I suppose. I did not sleep well."

Amelia's eyes narrowed, seeing through the excuse with ease. She had known Genevieve far too long to be so easily fooled. "It is him, isn't it? The marquess. I heard the rumours flying at the ball last night."

Genevieve's face heated as she dropped her gaze. She could hide nothing from Amelia, who had been her closest confidante since childhood. "There are always rumours," she said in a weak attempt at nonchalance.

"Do not pretend with me," Amelia said sternly. She sat beside Genevieve and grasped her hands. "You know you can tell me anything. I will not judge you, Genevieve. I only wish to help."

Genevieve's composure shattered at the kindness in her friend's voice. To her mortification, she felt tears pricking at her eyes. "Oh Amelia, I fear I have made a terrible mistake."

Amelia squeezed her hands. "How so?" she asked gently.

Genevieve took a shuddering breath. "I allowed myself to see beyond the rumours about Mordesley. To discover the man beneath the facade he presents to Society."

"And what did you discover?" Amelia prompted when she fell silent.

"He is not at all what I expected," Genevieve confessed in a rush. "He is intelligent, and kind, and makes me laugh in a way no one else does. When I'm with him, I feel…" She paused, struggling to find the words. "I feel free, as though I can be fully myself without pretence or judgment. There is a rare fragility to him beneath the surface."

Amelia's eyes widened. "You care for him greatly."

Genevieve nodded miserably. "Against all reason, I do. And now I find myself questioning everything I have been taught about duty and propriety." She looked at Amelia beseechingly. "How could something that feels so right be so wrong?"

"Oh Genevieve." Amelia gathered her into an embrace. "Perhaps what you have been taught is not as rigid as you believe. The heart wants what it wants, and love should never be wrong, as long as it is true."

Genevieve drew back to search her friend's face. "You cannot mean that. Defying one's duty to family and society for the sake of passion would be scandalous."

"I do not speak of passion alone," Amelia said. "But of finding a love that fortifies your spirit and gives you strength and comfort. If Mordesley is indeed worthy of your affections, perhaps this is a risk worth taking."

Genevieve stared at her, staggered by this perspective that flew in the face of all propriety. Yet somehow, in her heart, she knew Amelia spoke the truth. The seeds of doubt had been sown, and there would be no turning back. Her path was no longer clear, but for the first time, the unknown did not seem so fearful. She was no longer alone.

Genevieve bid Amelia farewell and made her way to the gardens for some solitude. Her mind was in turmoil, torn between duty and desire, propriety and passion.

She found a secluded bench and sat, closing her eyes as she breathed in the fresh scent of blooms. A vision of Sebastian came unbidden—his blue eyes alight with mirth, his smile slow and devastating. Her heart squeezed at the memory of his touch, the warmth of his embrace.

How could something so wrong feel so right?

She thought of her brother's words, and Amelia's. Perhaps there was truth in them, that love need not always follow the strict rules of society. Perhaps one could find fulfilment beyond the expectations and judgments of others.

Chapter Eleven

Sebastian sat in his study. A knock interrupted his brooding, and his butler entered upon being bid enter. "Pardon the intrusion, my lord, but Lady Constance is here requesting an audience. Shall I show her in?"

Sebastian tensed, immediately on guard. What could Constance want at this hour? Nothing good, he suspected, but refusing her entry would only stoke her pique. Better to allow the meeting, distasteful as it was bound to be, if only to hasten her departure.

"Send her in," he said resignedly.

Moments later, Constance swept into the study in a froth of silk and curls, looking far too pleased with herself. Sebastian remained seated, watching her warily.

"To what do I owe the unexpected pleasure, Lady Constance?"

Her smile turned coy as she drifted closer. "Must I have an excuse to call on an old friend? I hoped we might…reminisce, for old time's sake."

Sebastian suppressed a derisive snort. Reminisce indeed. More like prod at barely healed wounds, if past encounters were any indication. "As enjoyable as those sounds, I'm afraid I'm rather occupied at the moment—"

"With that little mouse, Lady Genevieve?" Constance interrupted, jealousy flashing in her eyes. "Don't think I haven't noticed your interest in her. Really Sebastian, I thought you had better taste."

Heat flooded Sebastian's cheeks at her words. He set down his glass with a thud, barely restraining a caustic retort. "My interests are none of your concern. I'll thank you not to speak ill of the lady."

Constance waved a dismissive hand. "Oh, come now, you cannot seriously be taken with her. She's dull as a post. Not to mention utterly ruined after that business with Avery. You have heard she broke of the engagement. I do not know why people keep allowing her to their balls." Her voice lowered to a purr as she perched on the arm of his chair. "Surely a virile man like yourself craves a woman of experience. One who knows how to please you?"

Sebastian shot to his feet, the heady scent of her cloying perfume suddenly sickening. "I think it's time you took your leave."

Pouting, Constance latched onto his arm. "Must you throw me out in the cold? Stay, we could have such fun together, like old times…"

Wrenching his arm free, Sebastian fixed her with an icy stare. "Let me make myself perfectly clear. There will be no rekindling between us. Goodnight, Lady Constance."

Her eyes blazed, mouth twisting into a spiteful sneer. "You will regret this insult, Mordesley," she hissed. "Mark my words."

With that, she spun on her heel and stormed out in a whirlwind of outrage. Sebastian watched her go, relief warring with disgust. Constance had always been petty and possessive, but this unprecedented bid to rekindle their affair bespoke a new level of desperation.

Well, she would find no willing victim in him. That part of his life was over. And if Constance insisted on harassing him further, he would not hesitate to take stronger measures to repel her unwanted advances.

Rubbing his eyes, Sebastian settled back into his chair with a weary sigh. He felt bone tired, emotionally wrung out after the day's turmoil and confrontations. Perhaps it was time to leave London for a spell, escape to his country estate where solitude might grant some peace.

At least there, the ghosts of the past could not follow. Or so he hoped.

The next evening found Sebastian ensconced in his private box at the opera, half-listening to the soaring aria while observing the glittering assemblage through his opera glasses. He had debated whether to attend the opening night performance but skipping it would allow further rumours of his supposed rakish behaviour. Better to put in a brief appearance and depart before gossipmongers could descend.

As he idly scanned over jewelled coiffures and elegant tailcoats, a flash of chestnut curls caught his attention. Heart quickening, he shifted the glasses.

Genevieve sat in the private box across the opera hall, a vision in azure silk. Sebastian admired the graceful line of her neck as she leaned forward, utterly enraptured by the performance unfolding onstage. Her obvious delight in the music brought a small smile to his lips.

As if sensing his gaze upon her, Genevieve chose that moment to glance across at his box. Their eyes locked and Sebastian felt the years slip away, the old connection between them kindling back to life. Genevieve's eyes widened in surprise, then she offered a tentative smile. Heart soaring, Sebastian started to rise, an invitation to pay call already forming on his lips—

A hand clapped down on his shoulder, jolting him from the moment. "There you are, Mordesley!" boomed Lord Drurie. "Hiding away in the shadows, you sly devil. You must join us below; the festivities have scarcely begun!"

Sebastian stifled an oath as Drurie bodily steered him from his box, the promise of speaking with Genevieve snatched away. But the image of her lingered, imprinted on his mind and heart. She had smiled at him. The game was not yet over between them. Hope flickered anew.

He managed to get as far as the quiet hallway behind the boxes before he heard. "My lord, wait!"

Sebastian turned with a scowl, prepared to rebuff whichever acquaintance had come to speak. But the sharp retort died on his lips as he beheld Lady Constance hastening toward him, wisps of hair escaping their elaborate style. Alarm stirred his gut at her dishevelled and distressed appearance. Glancing around he saw that they were alone in the hallway, Drurie having gone ahead and everyone else already moved off for intermission.

"My lady, what—"

"Oh Sebastian, it was dreadful!" Constance cried, pressing a hand to her bosom. "I can scarcely speak of it; I am so distraught…"

Sebastian grasped her shoulders, steadying her with effort. "Deep breaths,

Constance. Tell me what has happened."

She fanned herself, cheeks still flushed becomingly. "After you spurned my company last night, I was set upon by ruffians in the street! Oh, I feared for my life, sure I would meet my end in that dank alley…"

Unease prickled Sebastian's spine. "Go on," he said grimly.

"Well, they meant to rob me, I'm sure of it! But then you appeared from the shadows and fought them off like a hero from one of Mrs Radcliffe's novels." Her lashes fluttered. "I dare not think what would have become of me had you not been there…"

Sebastian stared at her incredulously as realisation struck. She meant to spin some fabricated tale of compromise, banking on rumours to force his hand and save her reputation. The audacity was staggering.

Taking her by the shoulders again, Sebastian met her gaze squarely. "I was at home all night, as my staff can verify. Nothing you claim passed between us, now or ever, nor will anyone believe otherwise." He felt a grudging pity at the spasm of thwarted rage that crossed her face. When it smoothed back into careful coyness, he sighed. "Let this go, Constance. Do not continue down this ruinous path, I beg you."

Her gaze turned venomous. "You reject me, yet pine after that whey-faced chit Genevieve. I will not stand for it!"

"Your jealousy blinds you." Sebastian gentled his grip, attempting diplomacy. "Return home and rest. No good will come of these wild accusations."

With that, he stepped back and made for the exit. This time, the footsteps that followed were not Constance's slippered tread, but the heavier fall of a man's boots. Unease prickled Sebastian's neck once more.

"One moment, Mordesley."

Sebastian turned slowly, muscles coiling. Lord Blaxland stood framed in the corridor, accusation in his flinty gaze. "Unhand my sister at once."

"My apologies, Lord Blaxland, but your sister came to me in her distress. I have done nothing untoward."

Blaxland's eyes narrowed, flickering between Sebastian and Constance. "I find that difficult to believe, given your reputation. My sister claims you accosted her after the opera last night."

Sebastian barely restrained an exasperated sigh. Of course, Constance would spin her web of lies to her brother now that her scheme had failed. "I can assure you; her allegations are false. I never laid a hand on her."

"Liar!" Constance cried, dabbing at her dry eyes with a handkerchief. "Are you calling me a wanton harlot who would invent such tales?"

Blaxland placed a protective arm around his sister. "I believe you, dear one. This scoundrel will answer for the insult."

Dread pooled in Sebastian's gut. Constance meant to see this through and force a confrontation. He raised his hands higher in supplication. "My lords, this is madness. I implore you, let us discuss this rationally before rash action is taken."

"The time for discussion is past," Blaxland snarled, hand dropping to the place where his sword would have sat at his hip had they been ready to duel. "You have dishonoured my sister. Prepare to face retribution."

Sebastian's heart sank even as his body tensed for defence. He had walked this path before, barely emerging with his life when Genevieve's brother had challenged him years ago. But he could not allow Constance's lies to steer him down that dark road again. Sebastian took a deep breath, willing his racing heart to steady. He could not allow this confrontation to escalate into violence. There had been enough pain and suffering already.

"My lord, I implore you - do not let anger cloud your judgment," he said evenly. "Whatever Lady Constance believes transpired; I give you my word of honour that I never accosted her. I ask that you search your heart and consider whether resorting to violence is truly the answer."

Lord Blaxland hesitated, doubt flickering across his features. Ever the diplomat, Sebastian pressed his advantage. "Come, let us retire downstairs and discuss this matter civilly over a drink. If Lady Constance still feels justice has not been served, we can revisit the issue with cooler heads prevail."

After a tense moment, Blaxland stepped back, his hand falling away from his sword. "Very well. We shall hear you out."

Sebastian released a silent breath of relief. With care and eloquence, he might yet talk them down from this disastrous course. "Thank you. I appreciate you giving me this chance to make my case." He turned to lead the way, catching Constance's eye as he did so. Her lips pressed into a thin line, thwarted malice smouldering in her gaze. This battle was far from over. But for now, diplomacy had won the day and violence had been averted.

As Sebastian strode down the corridor, the tension eased from his shoulders. He had escaped this particular trap, though Constance would surely lay more. Never again would he let his guard down around her. But that was a concern for the morrow. Tonight, he would savour his hard-won victory and the chance to clear his name through reason rather than bloodshed.

Lord Drurie appeared from round the corner "There you Mordesley! You were right behind me and then you were not. Lord Blaxland, you are here too old chap, and Lady Constance. Come, there is a small quartet setting up downstairs and people say they are fantastic. Though maybe you could show them a thing or two about music, eh Mordesley. I need another drink." Drurie swayed on the step indicating that he did not really need another drink. "Lady Constance! Do you think music is romantic? Apparently, music is romantic to women."

"It depends on who is playing and what they are playing Lord Drurie." Lady Constance turned her nose up and brushed past Drurie, clearly aiming to get away from the imbibed Lord.

Music as romantic, Sebastian mused. In that moment, he decided to host a private music recital at Mordesley House and invite Lady Genevieve and a select few others to hear him play. "Drurie, Lord Blaxland and I have a disagreement of sorts, will you hear us both out and see who correct?" Sebastian guided the two men after Lady Constance hoping to have the matter solved quickly.

Chapter Twelve

The velvet-padded invitation sat on Genevieve's vanity, seeming to taunt her with its bold, slanted script.

Sebastian had invited her to a private music recital at his estate. While the thought of an intimate evening listening to Sebastian play the violin stirred a flutter of anticipation in her breast.

Propriety dictated she refuse. As the eldest unmarried daughter of an earl, her reputation was her most valuable asset. Seen alone with a notorious rake like Sebastian, it would be irreparably damaged.

Still, curiosity gnawed at her. In public, Sebastian affected a cool detachment, but she sensed beneath his polished exterior lay hidden depths. What would be revealed in the music he chose to play? What emotions might slip past his usual restraint?

With a sigh, Genevieve moved to the window, gazing out at the garden below. The hydrangeas her mother so loved swayed in the breeze, a sea of pink and blue. She envied their simplicity, rooted as they were to one place. Her own path seemed tangled with thorns, duty and desire forever at odds.

Her fingers curled around the invitation as she wrestled with indecision. To go or not to go, that was the question. The consequences of either choice filled her with unease.

Staying home was the prudent option, yet it would mean an evening wondering what might have been. Risking her reputation to attend might lead to regret of a different sort. Sebastian Mordesley was not the kind of man one took lightly. There would be no going back if she stepped over the line of propriety into his world.

She sighed again, closing her eyes. The hydrangeas nodded their heads, as if in sympathy with her plight. Her heart and her head were at war, and try as she might, she could not find peace between them.

Genevieve opened her eyes and gazed once more at the invitation. The bold script seemed to shimmer and dance before her eyes, as elusive as the man who penned it. She knew not what she would choose, only that the path ahead would irrevocably change the course of her life. The moment balanced on a razor's edge, and she, powerless to stop it, could only wait and see which way she would fall.

She debated through the evening, weighing each choice until her head throbbed. She took to the gardens to clear her head. As darkness fell over the garden, her restless spirit kept pace. The hydrangeas slumbered as she paced between them, crushed petals marking her troubled steps.

When at last the mantel clock chimed midnight, Genevieve stood before her mirror and took a deep breath. She had made her decision.

* * *

The carriage arrived promptly at half past eight. Genevieve descended the steps in a rustle of cobalt damask silk, her pulse fluttering beneath lace gloves.

The carriage ride passed in a haze. She was only truly present again upon arriving at the estate, where a small gathering of society's elite milled about. Murmurs rippled through the crowd at her entrance. Sebastian met her at the door. He gave a curt nod the Gregory, her chaperone for the night.

"Forgive the short notice," he said. "I do hope you will enjoy the program."

"I look forward to being surprised, my lord."

A smile tugged at his lips. "Then I shall do my best not to disappoint."

He guided her to a seat near the front, solicitous as any perfect gentleman.

Only the smouldering look in his eyes betrayed the facade, hinting at the hidden depths within. Genevieve glanced away, heart pounding as the first notes of music began to play.

The performance was like nothing she had witnessed before. Sebastian's talent shone through each piece, raw with emotion and brimming with life. The music wove its spell around her, drawing her into a world of passion and longing. She was lost within its strains, awakened to joy and sorrow with each quiver of the violin.

When at last the final note faded, it was as waking from a dream. The applause and cheers seemed distant; her senses still caught in the melody's embrace. She turned to find Sebastian watching her, eyes soft with vulnerability in the dim light.

"Well?" he asked. "Did I surprise you?"

"Yes," she whispered. "Oh yes."

His smile lit like the dawn. "I am glad."

Sebastian guided her from the music room amidst congratulations from the other guests. Genevieve walked in a daze, clinging to the fading strains of melody inside her. Their feet guided them to a refreshments table.

"You truly enjoyed the performance," he said.

"How could I not?" She shook her head, at a loss for words. "You poured your heart and soul into the music. I have never experienced anything quite like it."

"Nor shall you ever again." His hand covered hers where it rested on the seat. "That piece was composed for you alone, my lady. A glimpse into the depths of my being, offered as a gift."

Tears pricked hot behind her eyes. She blinked them back, throat tightening. "Why?" she managed at last. "Why do you give me so much?"

"Because you deserve nothing less." His thumb stroked over her knuckles, a feather-light caress. "And because I find I cannot help myself when it comes to you." Someone called his name from the other side of the room. "You must excuse me as I see to my other guests."

Then he was gone, leaving her alone with the memory of music and the ache of longing in her heart.

Genevieve lingered in the foyer, reluctant to move. Sebastian's parting words echoed through her mind as the faint strains of melody lingered at the edges of her hearing.

She closed her eyes, transported back to the intimacy of the music room. The soft glow of candlelight, the hush of anticipation as he tuned his instrument. Then the first silvery notes had spilled into the air, pure and true as starlight.

A shiver ran down her spine at the recollection. Never had she imagined such beauty could exist in this world, or that she might be so profoundly stirred. Every note had seemed to strike a chord within her, awakening a tumult of feelings as if from a long slumber.

Joy and sorrow intertwined, longing and regret. A wild, impossible hope she dared not name. And beneath it all, a deepening ache she now recognised as the desire to give Sebastian all that he had given her. To bare her soul as he had done and offer him the gift of herself in return.

Madness. She pressed a hand to her chest, as if she could quell the riotous beat of her heart through sheer force of will. What was she thinking? She could not seriously consider initiating a romantic attachment with a man of Sebastian's reputation. However tender or noble his actions might seem; he was still a rake at his core. Any relationship between them would surely end in ruin.

With a sigh, she turned toward the door and her carriage. She would not think of Sebastian or the feelings he evoked tonight. She would retire to her room, read a book until her eyes grew heavy, and pray for a dreamless sleep to restore her senses.

In the morning, she would be Genevieve St. Claire once more - a woman of poise and propriety, not a creature of reckless passion. And she would put this night, and all its impossible fancies, firmly out of her mind.

As she reached the carriage, the crunch of gravel sounded behind her. "Genevieve, wait." She turned to find Sebastian striding towards her, his usual nonchalant facade replaced by an expression of raw longing. Without preamble he took her face in his hands, his thumbs gently caressing her cheeks.

"Forgive me, but I cannot let you leave tonight without knowing the truth." His voice was low and fervent. "From the moment we met, you have haunted me. No other woman has challenged and intrigued me as you do. I made a mistake 5 years ago, I was young. I'm sorry." Genevieve's pulse quickened at his words; spoken with an urgency she had never heard from him before.

"Being with you like this, I can finally be myself rather than the rake they all presume me to be." His eyes searched hers, revealing a glimpse of the vulnerability behind his polished exterior. "Tell me if you feel the same, if there is a chance you could love me as I love you."

Genevieve saw the sincerity of his words reflected in his face. Her breath caught in her throat, the rest of the world fading away until there was only Sebastian. Throwing caution aside, she wrapped her arms around his neck and pulled him into a fervent kiss.

At first, he went still, stunned by her boldness. Then with a muffled groan he was kissing her back, his mouth hot and hungry against hers. She twined her fingers through his hair, thrilled at the feel of his strong arms wrapping tightly around her as though he would never let go.

When at last they broke apart, Sebastian kept her clasped close, his brow pressed against hers.

"My dear, reckless Genevieve," he murmured, a wondering smile curving his kiss-swollen lips. "You have laid me bare."

She caressed the nape of his neck, desire and affection welling powerfully within her breast. "As you have me, Sebastian."

He kissed her again, more tenderly this time, a promise of passionate days yet to come. Genevieve melted into his embrace, her last shreds of doubt burning away like mist under the rising sun. With Sebastian, she was finally home.

The next morning, Genevieve awoke to sunlight streaming through the windows of her bedchamber. For a moment, she blinked in confusion at the surroundings before memories of the previous evening came flooding back: the private recital, Sebastian's music and poetry intertwining as he bared his soul to her, their growing closeness culminating in a kiss of searing passion. Heat suffused her cheeks as she recalled the intimacy they had shared, her reservations melting away in the face of his ardour and sincerity. She had revealed herself to him in turn, and she had found no cause for regret. Only joy. And longing. And a bone-deep certainty that she had made the right choice in trusting him with her heart.

Genevieve rose from the bed and rang for her maid, contemplating how she might confess these new developments to her dearest friend. Amelia had always encouraged her to follow her heart, but this went against all dictates of propriety. Yet she could not find it within herself to regret her actions. Sebastian had vowed to make her his in truth, and she believed him. They would face the consequences of their choices together, let Society think what it may.

When her maid arrived, Genevieve instructed her to send for Lady Amelia at her earliest convenience. She had a tale to share that would no doubt shock and scandalize, but Amelia would understand. Of all people, she would understand. And she would rejoice to see Genevieve's heart at last set free. Amelia swept into Genevieve's drawing room an hour later, concern etched into her delicate features. "My dear friend, what is it? Your note said it was a matter of some urgency."

Genevieve rose to greet her, smiling in a way she knew would set Amelia instantly on edge. "Thank you for coming. I have something of a confession to make."

Amelia's eyes widened. She knew Genevieve too well not to anticipate something thoroughly improper. "Oh? Do tell."

"My dear Amelia, you must promise not to judge me too harshly. When Lord Sebastian walked me to my carriage last night, he…he kissed me! I know it was shockingly improper, but in that moment, I was helpless to resist." Genevieve said without preamble. Better to deliver the news swiftly, like tearing off a bandage. "We have declared our love for one another, and while he has not yet proposed marriage, I have every faith he shall."

For several moments Amelia simply stared, too stunned to speak. Then she sank into a chair, pressing a hand to her chest. "Genevieve, this is … oh, this is disastrous. Have you any idea the damage to your reputation should this become known?"

"I am well aware of the risks," Genevieve said. "But I love him, Amelia, with all my heart. I will face any consequences to be with him, even if it means turning my back on Society and all I have ever known."

Amelia was silent, her expression torn between concern for her friend's wellbeing and joy at the love blossoming between two souls meant to be together. "Does he love you as well?" she asked at last. "Can you be certain he will do right by you in the end?"

"Yes," Genevieve said with quiet conviction. "He has vowed to make me his wife, to spend his life proving how much I mean to him. I trust him to keep his word."

After a long moment, Amelia rose and embraced her. "Then I shall trust in your judgment and wish you both every happiness. You deserve nothing less."

Genevieve hugged her close, tears of gratitude and relief burning her eyes. She had feared Amelia's censure, but true friendship proved stronger than mere rules of etiquette.

"Thank you," she whispered, and Amelia squeezed her tighter in response. "Follow your heart, dearest," she said. "It will never lead you astray."

Amelia took her leave after some tea and much gossip. Genevieve knew that Amelia did not approve but wished her friend happiness. Amelia was not aware of her and Sebastian's dalliance 5 years prior. Only Gregory knew, and she worried how he might take it.

What would her parents say when she told them of her intention to marry Sebastian? They had always warned her against his carefree and rebellious ways, believing him an unsuitable match for their dutiful daughter. Would they forbid the union? The thought filled her with anguish. She did not wish to lose her family, but neither could she give up Sebastian now that she had found love and acceptance in his arms. She took a deep breath and headed downstairs.

Her mother greeted her in the parlour, brows knitting with concern at Genevieve's uncharacteristically distracted air. "Is something amiss, dear one?"

Genevieve clasped her hands to hide their trembling. "Mother, I have something of grave importance to discuss with you and Father."

Alarm flickered in her mother's eyes, but she nodded. "Come, let us speak in the drawing room."

Genevieve followed, her heart pounding as she contemplated the events that were about to unfold. The path before her was fraught with obstacles, but if love truly did conquer all, she had faith that she and Sebastian would prevail. Their future was uncertain, but as long as they faced it together, she knew in her soul that all would be well.

In the drawing room, Genevieve's father looked up from his book with a frown. "What is this about, Penelope? Has something happened?"

Genevieve cleared her throat, clasping her hands tighter to mask their trembling. "Father, Mother, I have come to a decision about my future." Her voice was scarcely more than a whisper. "I intend to accept Sebastian's proposal of marriage."

There was a heavy silence. Genevieve's father set his book aside, lips pressed into a thin line. "I see. And have you given any thought to the consequences of such an unsuitable match?" His tone was filled with concern for her.

Genevieve lifted her chin. "Sebastian may not be a traditional choice, but he is a good man. He loves me, and I love him in return. I do not wish to spend my life devoid of love and passion for the sake of propriety."

"You would throw away your reputation for the fleeting fancies of romance?" Her father shook his head. "You are not thinking clearly, Genevieve. Once you are married, there will be no going back. Are you prepared to face the whispers?"

"I care not for the opinions of those who would judge me for following my heart," she said softly. "Sebastian and I shall build a life together filled with joy and meaning, whatever may come."

Lady Penelope took Genevieve's hands in her own, gaze imploring. "My darling, we only wish for your happiness and security. The path you are choosing will be difficult. Can you truly say you are ready to face such hardship for love?"

Genevieve gave her mother's hands a gentle squeeze. "I can, and I shall. My place is by Sebastian's side, and nothing anyone says or does will change my mind." She smiled, a flush of peace descending upon her. "Fear not, for I go into this with eyes open. As long as we have each other, all will be well."

Her parents exchanged a long, inscrutable look. At length, her father sighed and rose to his feet. He came forward and enfolded Genevieve in a strong embrace.

"You are your mother's daughter, through and through," he said gruffly. "Once you have set your mind to something, nothing can sway you. I pray you prove us wrong in this and find the happiness you seek." He held her at arm's length, eyes glinting. "Now, I suppose we had best prepare to welcome the new Marquess into the family."

Joy and relief flooded Genevieve's heart. She threw her arms around her father, tears of gratitude spilling down her cheeks. It seemed love truly had conquered all, and her future with Sebastian was finally assured. Her path was clear. Now all that remained was to tell Sebastian of her decision and begin their future together.

Chapter Thirteen

Sebastian paced the length of his study, unable to keep still. The memory of Genevieve in his arms last night still burned brightly in his mind, along with the sweetness of her kiss. He had borne his soul and she had accepted him, faults and all. Now his heart yearned to make her his in truth. But he knew he must tread carefully. While Genevieve seemed receptive to his advances, she was a lady of status. He would need to court her properly and gain her family's approval before any talk of betrothal.

With a sigh, Sebastian moved to his desk and scribbled out a note to his solicitor requesting a meeting. There wcrc settlements and contracts to be drawn up, finances and properties to be sorted. He wanted to provide Genevieve with comfort and security, to prove himself worthy of the precious gift of her hand.

A knock interrupted his thoughts. "A letter for you, my lord," the butler said upon entering.

Sebastian took the proffered envelope, frowning when he recognised his aunt's florid handwriting. Her shrill disapproval still stung from their last correspondence regarding his courtship with Genevieve. But he could not ignore a summons from his only remaining family.

He scanned the letter quickly, brows drawing together. His aunt's usual gossip and complaints were replaced with an urgent request for him to travel to her estate at once regarding a "family matter of some delicacy."

Sebastian crumpled the missive in his fist, dread pooling in his stomach. His aunt was ever one for histrionics and fabricated scandal. Still, he could not dismiss her cryptic message entirely. With a muttered oath, he rang for his valet to prepare for immediate travel.

It seemed sharing his hopes with Genevieve would need to wait. Family duty called, much as he chafed at the delay. But once this tiresome business with his aunt was concluded, he would return and make Genevieve his, propriety be damned. She was his future, the missing piece he had searched for all his life. A few more weeks of waiting was a small price to pay for a lifetime of happiness by her side.

With Genevieve in his thoughts and her kiss still lingering upon his lips, Sebastian strode out the door and into the night. The sooner he resolved this, the sooner he could claim his heart's desire.

The carriage rolled through the countryside, miles passing in a blur as Sebastian made haste to his aunt's estate. His thoughts drifted to Genevieve, as they so often did these days. Her sweet smile, her keen wit, the warmth of her in his arms…he yearned to hold her again, to kiss her smiling lips and hear her passionate sighs. Soon, he told himself. Once this business with his aunt was seen to, he could return to London and make the lady his bride.

Eventually the carriage turned down the long drive leading to his aunt's manor home. Sebastian gritted his teeth, mentally girding himself for the impending unpleasantness. No doubt his aunt had concocted some gross exaggeration to compel his presence. Well, he would indulge her theatrics, if only to speed his return to the woman who occupied his every thought.

His aunt met him in her lavishly decorated parlour, a handkerchief clutched in one trembling hand. "Oh, Sebastian! Thank heavens you've come."

Sebastian sighed. "What seems to be the matter, Aunt? Your letter indicated some urgent family crisis."

"Indeed, it is dreadful!" His aunt collapsed onto a chaise, waving her handkerchief dramatically. "You must help me, Sebastian. My honour and good name have been called into question! Only you, as head of this family, can defend me."

Sebastian pinched the bridge of his nose, impatience simmering beneath his calm facade. "Just tell me plainly, what is this all about?"

His aunt sniffled into her handkerchief. "That dreadful Viscountess Balmer has spread lies, claiming I tried to sabotage her daughter's engagement. You must call her out and defend my honour!"

"How so aunt? Do you wish me to duel the woman?"

"Do not be silly Sebastian! Oh, but there must be something you can do! Have her husband stripped of his titles or something."

With monumental effort, Sebastian restrained a scathing retort. Duels and feuds were the stuff of hot-headed youths, not grown men with far better uses for their time. He had a future to build with Genevieve, and no patience left for his aunt's histrionics.

"I will speak with the viscountess and sort this out civilly," he said shortly. "There is no need for rash action. Now if you'll excuse me, I must rest before returning to London in the morning."

Ignoring his aunt's squawking protests, Sebastian hastened to his guest room and shut the door firmly. This pointless detour had delayed his return to Genevieve long enough. It was time he left behind theatrics and devoted himself to securing the future that truly mattered - one with the woman he loved faithfully by his side.

The next morning, Sebastian bid his aunt a brisk farewell despite her entreaties for him to remain. His thoughts were already racing ahead to London, to Genevieve, as the carriage hurried down the long drive.

He had tarried here long enough. It was time to return and continue his courtship in earnest. There were contracts to be negotiated, announcements to be made. A wedding to plan, God willing. His heartbeat faster at the thought.

The miles seemed to crawl by at a snail's pace. Sebastian rapped his cane restlessly against the floor, urging the horses on faster. He had wasted enough time on pointless distractions. Now his focus must be on securing his future with Genevieve. And he would let nothing else distract him from making Genevieve his bride. She was his anchor, his purpose, his heart's true home. With her by his side, the future could hold nothing but joy.

On returning home from his unnecessary trip to the country, Sebastian found an invitation to a ball that evening waiting for him. After a few discrete enquiries, he found that both Lady Genevieve and the viscountess' daughter, Miss Alexandra Balmer would be in attendance. He could fix his aunt's indiscretions and see Genevieve all in one night.

Chapter Fourteen

The rustling of crinoline skirts and the low murmur of polite conversation drifted through the crowded ballroom as Genevieve gazed out at the swirling sea of dancers. Her younger sister Georgina floated across the dancefloor in the arms of Lord Frederick Ainsford, her cheeks flushed and eyes shining as Frederick whispered in her ear.

Genevieve bit back a wistful sigh, her gloved fingers tightening around the glass of punch in her hand. She longed to lose herself in the music and movement as Georgina had, swept away by a handsome partner in a whirl of colour and joy. But no gentleman had yet approached her this evening, and her chances of capturing Sebastian's attention seemed slim. He had arrived late and scarcely glanced her way, his piercing blue eyes scanning the room before settling on a vivacious young woman in a revealing scarlet gown.

Georgina drifted closer on Ainsford's arm, still dancing, her face alight with happiness. "Oh, is it not a splendid ball? And is not Lord Ainsford the most wonderful dancer?"

Genevieve summoned a smile. "Indeed. I am glad you are enjoying yourself."

"Are you not having any luck, dearest?" Georgina glanced around the room, her brow furrowing. "I have not seen Lord Mordesley approach you yet."

"I am sure he is merely preoccupied." Genevieve waved a dismissive hand, though unease coiled in the pit of her stomach. She longed to confide her worries in Georgina but refused to dampen her sister's spirits. "Go, continue your dancing. I shall be quite content here."

"If you are certain..." Georgina hesitated, reaching out from the dance floor to squeeze her arm. "Chin up, Genevieve. The evening is still young."

Genevieve nodded and watched Georgina float back into Ainsford's arms, a vision in rose silk and flushed contentment. Sighing, she turned her gaze once more to the swirling dancers, determined to maintain her poise even as longing and doubt warred within her. The flickering candlelight cast shadows that seemed to echo the unease in her heart, and she clutched at the fraying threads of hope that Sebastian might yet ask her to dance.

The music drifted to a close, and Geevieve glimpsed Sebastian across the room, his handsome features etched with a frown. His gaze swept the crowd and came to rest on her, and for a moment her breath caught at the unguarded emotion in his eyes. Then the crowd shifted, and he disappeared from view.

Genevieve blinked back the sting of tears, mortified at her reaction. She was being foolish—there were any number of reasons Sebastian had not asked her to dance. He was likely occupied with his social obligations, or—

"Forgive me for keeping you waiting, my lady."

She started at the sound of his voice, low and intimate at her ear, and turned to find him bowing before her, eyes glinting with warmth. "I trust you will do me the honour of this dance?"

Joy flooded Genevieve's veins, banishing her doubts. "It would be my pleasure, Lord Mordesley."

His hand closed around hers, firm and sure, as he led her onto the floor. They fell into an easy rhythm, Sebastian's movements graceful and confident. Genevieve peered up at him through her lashes, uncertain how to broach the subject of his earlier absence.

"You seemed quite occupied this evening," she began. "Enjoying the company of your many admirers, I'm sure."

"On the contrary." His eyes darkened. "I found myself quite unable to enjoy anything until I could ask you to dance."

"Truly?" Genevieve blinked; sure, she had misheard him.

"In truth, I was detained by a trifling matter that my aunt foisted upon me.

I feared the delay might lead you to doubt my affections, and for that I can only apologise." His hand tightened around hers. "You must know that you are the only woman who occupies my thoughts this evening."

Genevieve's cheeks warmed at his words. "You are too bold, my lord."

"Am I?" His lips curved into a smile. "When it comes to you, my lady, I cannot seem to help myself."

She averted her gaze, unsure how to respond to his frank admiration. In the silence, she became aware of the gentle pressure of his hand at her waist, the steadiness of his gaze, the faint scent of sandalwood that clung to his jacket. Her pulse quickened as she struggled to find her voice.

"People speak of your past, you know," she said at last. "Your reputation precedes you."

"Ah yes, my 'reputation.'" His jaw tightened. "I cannot deny my past mistakes. I was a foolish young man who squandered his youth and betrayed the trust of many. I do not ask you to overlook my sins."

"And yet you seem very different now." Genevieve searched his face, struck by the sincerity in his tone. "Almost as though you are trying to make amends for past wrongs."

"You are perceptive." Sebastian's eyes softened. "The truth is, I have been trying to redeem myself these last years. To regain my honour and prove myself worthy of respect once more. It has been a slow process, but I find myself caring more for duty and propriety now than frivolous pleasures."

"I see." Genevieve considered his words, recalling the evidence of change she had observed in him. The conscientiousness with which he approached his responsibilities. His generosity toward tenants and servants.

The music slowed, and Sebastian drew her closer. "Can you find it in your heart to forgive me, Genevieve, as I have tried to forgive myself? To see the man I am now, rather than the fool I once was?"

She gazed up at him, stirred by the vulnerability in his expression. The last of her doubts crumbled away, replaced by a deepening tenderness and the conviction that love, like redemption, was possible for those who sought it in earnest.

"Yes," she whispered. "I believe I can."

His answering smile lit his eyes with quiet joy. As the final notes of the song drifted around them, Genevieve rested her head on his shoulder, content in the knowledge that she had made the right choice. Sebastian's grip tightened around her, wordless understanding passing between them as the world faded away, leaving only this moment of new beginnings.

The next day, Genevieve wandered the public gardens, her thoughts tumbling over one another as wildly as the roses that lined the path. The remnants of last night's ball still lingered—the music, the dancing, Sebastian's admission.

She paused beside a marble fountain, tracing her fingers over its cool, smooth edge. Droplets of water splashed and trickled, the rhythmic sounds echoing the beat of her heart.

He had borne his soul to her in a way she had not thought him capable of. The façade of charming indifference had cracked, giving way to a vulnerability that had shaken her even as it drew her in.

And she had forgiven him. Whispered the words against his shoulder, meaning them with all her heart.

Yet now, in the light of day, old doubts crept in. The lingering spectres of his reputation and her duty, shadows she could not quite banish. He had yet to ask her hand in marriage.

She sighed, gripping the fountain's edge. Last night, it had all seemed so simple. A chance at love and redemption, a new beginning born of shared understanding. But could it truly be so easy? To cast aside the expectations of Society and forge her own path? To risk scandal and censor for the love of a man whose past was marked by careless indulgence.

Her heart gave one answer, while her head supplied another. And between them, Genevieve could find no peace.

A rustle of silk skirts drew Genevieve from her reverie. She glanced up to find Lady Constance approaching, a cascade of rose-pink satin and blonde curls.

Genevieve stiffened, fingers tightening around the fountain. She and Lady Constance had once been friends, but that was before the woman had set her sights on Sebastian. Now there was a brittle tension between them, all barbed smiles and veiled insults.

"Lady Genevieve." Constance's voice was sweet, but her eyes held a predatory gleam. "Enjoying the gardens, are we?"

Genevieve inclined her head. "The weather is lovely today."

"Indeed." Constance drifted closer, regarding Genevieve through half-lidded eyes. "Though not quite as lovely as the ball last evening, I think. So many handsome gentlemen, and eager to dance with any lady fortunate enough to catch their eye." Her gaze sharpened. "Any lady not otherwise preoccupied, that is."

Heat rose in Genevieve's cheeks. So, Constance had noticed her dance with Sebastian. She should not have expected otherwise.

Squaring her shoulders, she met the other woman's stare. "Fortunate indeed," she echoed. "To find a gentleman with whom one shares a true connection."

Constance's smile tightened, but she waved a dismissive hand. "Oh, come now, you can hardly think Lord Mordesley sees you as anything more than a passing fancy? His attentions are as changeable as the weather, there one moment and gone the next. I should hate to see you pine away for a man who will never offer you anything of substance."

Genevieve's fingers curled into fists, nails biting into her palms. How dare she? As if she knew anything of Sebastian's feelings or what might lie between them. She drew a sharp breath, wrestling her anger back under control. There would be no satisfying Constance, no way to convince her of the truth. But Genevieve need not justify herself to this woman.

"Your concern is misplaced," she said, icy calm. "But I thank you for your solicitude, however insincere it may be."

"Come now, there's no need to be rude. I am only thinking of your reputation—and your poor sister's. It would be a shame if word got out that the St. Claire girls were not as...pristine, shall we say, as everyone believes."

Heat flooded Genevieve's cheeks. "How dare you. Your threats mean nothing; everyone knows what sort of woman you are."

"Do they?" Constance purred. "I wonder. All it would take is a few whispers in the right ears, a hint of scandal, to ruin you both forever." Her gaze was hard as flint. "The choice is yours, Lady St. Claire. Give up your little dalliance with the marquess or suffer the consequences".

Genevieve's heart was pounding so loudly she could barely think. But she grasped at the shreds of her courage and looked Constance square in the eye.

"I will not be bullied by you. And neither will Mordesley; he sees you for what you truly are. Your bitterness shames you far more than any rumour ever could."

Constance's eyes blazed. For a moment Genevieve thought she might strike her. But she only smiled again, colder than a winter frost.

"You'll regret those words, Lady Genevieve. Someday very soon, you will regret them with all your heart." She glided past Genevieve to the fountain, dipping her fingers in. "The choice is yours. But know this: you have now made an enemy of me. And I never give up what is mine."

Try as she might to maintain a dignified composure, Genevieve found her resolve crumbling; "Good day Lady Constance." She turned on her heel and walked out of the gardens.

Genevieve glanced back to see Constance's hands twisted in the silk of her gown, crushing the delicate fabric as she sought an outlet for her frustration.

The next day, Genevieve sat in a seclude part of the public gardens, watching the ducks drift across the pond. The peaceful setting did little to calm her restless spirit, but she had needed an escape from the clamour of London. Here, at least, she could think. Sebastian found her there some time later. He approached quietly, but she sensed his presence and turned to meet his gaze. The concern in his eyes made her heart ache with tenderness.

"I heard about your encounter with Constance, from Lord Henry who witnessed it" he said. "Are you quite all, right?"

"As well as can be expected." She attempted a smile, but it felt brittle. "Your concern is touching, my lord, but unnecessary. I will not allow her spite to distress me."

"Brave words, but I see the truth in your face." Sebastian sat beside her, taking one of her hands in his. "My darling, do not pretend with me. I know how deeply she wounded you."

His gentle tone undid her. To her dismay, hot tears welled in her eyes and spilled down her cheeks. Mortified, she tried to pull away, but Sebastian drew her into his arms.

"Hush, my love," he murmured, stroking her hair. "Do not hide from me. I am here to comfort you."

She wept against his chest, clinging to him. His embrace was her refuge, his love her shelter in the storm. Constance could threaten and accuse all she liked, but she could not shake Genevieve's faith in the man who held her now.

When her tears were spent, she drew back to find Sebastian watching her with a tenderness that stole her breath. He brushed a curl back from her face, his knuckles skimming her cheek.

"You are so dear to me," he said softly. "Nothing Constance does or says will ever change that. Our love is stronger than her malice, Genevieve." He smiled, glanced about to make sure they were alone and touched his lips to hers. "Have faith, my darling. All will be well."

His kiss and his words kindled a spark of hope in her heart. Together, they could face any challenge and emerge triumphant. She had only to trust in him, and in their love. With Sebastian by her side, she could be brave.

Genevieve gazed up at Sebastian, her eyes shining with affection. "You are my strength, my heart, my everything," she whispered. "As long as we are together, no obstacle is insurmountable."

A smile lit Sebastian's face. He stroked her cheek, his touch igniting sparks along her skin. "Then together we shall remain, my love, today and always."

His lips descended to hers again, soft yet passionate. Genevieve melted into his embrace, losing herself in the sweetness of his kiss. When they parted, she was breathless, her cheeks flushed with warmth.

Sebastian's eyes gleamed at the sight. "You are exquisite when you blush," he said, tucking a stray curl behind her ear. "But lovelier still when you smile. Will you not smile for me, Genevieve?"

She laughed, a burst of joy escaping her. "You ridiculous man! Must you always tease me so?"

"I cannot help myself," he said, grinning. "Your reactions are far too delightful. Teasing you brings me great joy."

Genevieve swatted his arm, though she could not suppress her smile. "You vex me terribly at times."

"And yet you love me still," Sebastian said, pulling her close again.

"Despite your vexing ways," she admitted. "Or perhaps because of them."

"I shall have to vex you more often, then." Sebastian's eyes gleamed with mischief. "If it wins me your affections, the trouble will be well worth it."

Genevieve shook her head, a smile playing about her lips. "You have already won my affections, vexing man that you are. There is no need for further troublemaking."

"Is that so?" Sebastian's voice softened. "Then I shall have to find new ways to please you instead."

A blush rose in Genevieve's cheeks at his intimate tone. She averted her gaze, her heart fluttering. "Sebastian…"

He tilted her chin up, his eyes searching hers. "What is it, my love? You know you can tell me anything."

Drawing a breath, Genevieve steeled her nerves. She had to be honest with him, to bare her heart as he had borne his to her.

"I fear…" She hesitated, cheeks burning. "That is, I worry that I may not please you as a wife should. I have had no experience in such matters, and—"

"Hush, beloved." Sebastian's eyes were tender. "You need not worry about that."

"But I do," she said. "You deserve a wife who can give you everything you desire. I fear I may fall short of your expectations. I worry that you desire someone such as Lady Constance."

"The only thing I desire is your love," Sebastian said. "As for the rest, we shall learn and grow together. I want you as you are, Genevieve, innocent or experienced. My love for you depends not on what you can give me, but simply on the fact that you are you."

Tears pricked Genevieve's eyes at his heartfelt words. "Truly?" she whispered.

"Truly." Sebastian kissed her softly. "You are the love of my life, Genevieve, and that shall never change. Do not doubt yourself, or my affections. There is no obstacle we cannot face together."

Genevieve clung to him, overwhelmed by joy and relief. She had borne her heart to him, and he had accepted her as she was. With Sebastian by her side, she felt she could overcome any challenge. His love gave her courage and strength, a shield against her fears and doubts.

United, there was no obstacle they could not surmount. And together, they would face each new experience with open hearts and willing spirits, learning and growing as one.

The next morning, Genevieve awoke to find a single red rose had been delivered to the house. A note was attached, penned in Sebastian's elegant scrawl:

My dearest Genevieve,

A rose to signify my love, which shall bloom more brightly each day we are together. I count the moments until I see your sweet face again.

Yours always,
Sebastian

Genevieve clutched the rose to her breast, blinking back happy tears. Sebastian's thoughtfulness and affection never ceased to amaze her. With him, she felt cherished and adored in a way she had never known before.

A knock at the parlour door interrupted her bliss. Expecting her lady's maid, Genevieve bid the visitor entrance. To her surprise, Lady Constance swept into the room, a sly smile on her painted lips.

"Good morning, Lady Genevieve," she purred. "I trust you slept well? I wondered if you had heard the latest on dits making the rounds."

Genevieve stiffened, immediately on guard. Whatever news Lady Constance brought would not be pleasant. She had not forgotten the woman's attempts to ruin Sebastian and did not doubt she meant them harm.

"I have not," Genevieve said coolly. "But I doubt it is of any interest to me."

"Oh, but this concerns your dear Marquess," Lady Constance said. "It seems Mordesley's reputation is not as reformed as you had hoped. There are whispers of late-night carousals and a certain opera dancer he has been squiring about town."

Genevieve's heart clenched, but she kept her expression neutral. "And what proof have you of these claims?" she asked. "Or are they merely the bitter imaginings of a jealous and spiteful woman? I do believe you were seen at the opera with him not that long ago, maybe it is your reputation at stake."

Lady Constance's cheeks flushed an unbecoming shade of red. "How dare you!" she exclaimed. "I am only telling you this as a friend, so you do not make a fool of yourself over a man like Mordesley."

"We are not friends," Genevieve said coldly. "And I do not believe your lies. Now if you will excuse me, I have more important matters to attend to."

She strode to the door and held it open, staring pointedly at Lady Constance. With an indignant huff, the woman swept out of the room in a flurry of silk skirts.

Genevieve shut the door and leaned against it, sighing in relief. Lady Constance's schemes would not succeed. Her faith in Sebastian was unshakeable, their bond tempered by trust. Together, they would overcome each new obstacle, emerging stronger than before. And Lady Constance would not rest until she accepted that her jealousy and malice could not defeat them.

The next day, Genevieve sat by the window in her private parlour, gazing out at the well-manicured gardens below. Her thoughts drifted to Sebastian, as they often did these days. Despite Lady Constance's venomous words, her conviction in his goodness had only deepened.

There were glimpses of his past that still remained shrouded in mystery, but what she did know spoke volumes about the man he had become. He was kind and compassionate, witty yet wise, noble in bearing and gentle in spirit. The more time they spent together, the more she came to appreciate each new facet of his complex and multi-dimensional character.

Society may have been quick to judge him for the sins of his youth, but Genevieve saw beyond the superficial. She knew with a certainty that echoed in her bones that Sebastian Mordesley was a man redeemed, his honour restored, his heart open once more to love and joy and laughter.

A soft smile curved her lips as she gazed out the window. The sun dipped lower in the sky, its golden light filtering through the trees. She thought of

Sebastian's eyes, warm and brown and full of affection when he looked at her. Her heart swelled with tenderness at the memory. No matter what obstacles were placed in their path, her love for him would endure. The bonds between them were woven of trust and understanding, compassion and care. Together they would face each new challenge and emerge stronger, their commitment to one another deepening with every trial overcome.

Lady Constance's schemes would not prevail. Genevieve's conviction in Sebastian was unshakeable, her faith in their love as constant as the sunrise. She knew, with a certainty that resonated in her soul, that he was the missing piece that made her whole, the light that brightened even the darkest of days. And she would cherish each moment they shared, through joy and through sorrow, today and forevermore. The sun dipped below the horizon, shadows lengthening across the room. Genevieve rose from her seat by the window and lit a candle, the flickering flame casting a warm glow over the space.

She thought again of Sebastian and felt a surge of affection. Despite the obstacles they had faced, their connection had only grown deeper. The bonds between them were woven of far more than fleeting passion or superficial delight. They had built a foundation of trust and understanding, a refuge where they could be fully known and loved.

With Sebastian at her side, Genevieve felt as though she could face any challenge. His love gave her strength and courage, helping her to see beyond the limits others tried to place upon her. He embraced her fully for who she was, scars and imperfections included, and cherished each part of her soul.

No matter what anyone else might say, Genevieve knew the truth. Sebastian Mordesley was a man of honour and integrity, compassion and care. He had overcome his past mistakes through hard-won wisdom and a commitment to become a better man. The love they shared was genuine, a bond to stand the test of time.

She smiled softly, warmth flooding her chest. However, much Lady Constance might scheme and sabotage, she could not shake Genevieve's conviction. Their love was stronger than any obstacle, enduring beyond all trials. Genevieve had found her heart's true home in Sebastian's arms, and together they would brave each new challenge with courage and hope.

Chapter Fifteen

Sebastian paced the length of his study, raking a hand through his hair in frustration. The solicitor had just departed after giving him distressing news - there were complications with the marriage contracts that would delay the wedding for several weeks at least. Hidden debts tied to some ancestral Mordesley properties required untangling before the financial arrangements with the St. Claires could be formalised.

Sebastian cursed under his breath. The delay was untenable. Having confessed their love, he and Genevieve were eager to make their union official. These endless legal technicalities were maddening obstacles keeping them apart. He could not ask for her hand until they were sorted.

A knock interrupted his brooding. "A letter for you, my lord," his butler announced upon entering. "From Lady Lavinia."

Sebastian frowned as he took the proffered envelope. His aunt was the last person he wished to hear from right now. Her previous letters had been filled with dire warnings about the impropriety of his match with Genevieve. Her last calling him to her estate surely an attempt to distance him from Genevieve. This latest missive would no doubt contain more of the same unwanted opinions.

With a sigh, Sebastian broke the seal and quickly scanned the contents, his frown deepening with each line. Just as he'd expected, Aunt Lavinia urged him to reconsider his engagement, citing Genevieve's "dubious past" and "unsuitability as a marchioness." As if he would cast Genevieve aside based on the petty judgments of close-minded aristocrats, though none of it true.

Sebastian crumpled the letter in his fist, prepared to ignore his aunt's tiresome meddling. Then a signature at the bottom caught his eye - Lord Eustace Merryweather. Ice crept down Sebastian's spine. Lord Merryweather was one of his most influential peers in Parliament and notorious for adhering to tradition. If he sided with Aunt Lavinia's position...

Jaw clenched; Sebastian tossed the letter atop his desk. This could present real trouble. Lord Merryweather's disapproval may well sway other members against his marriage and thus kill any bills he wished to put through parliament. Combined with the latest legal obstacles, the forces conspiring to separate him from Genevieve seemed insurmountable.

Restless energy propelled Sebastian to his feet. He needed air to clear his head and give him time to strategize a solution. Storming out the front doors, he barely registered the concerned inquiries of the staff as he passed. Right now, his thoughts were consumed with only one thing - finding a way back to Genevieve.

The brisk air helped settle Sebastian's churning mind as he strode through the bustling streets of Mayfair. He forced himself to focus on each problem methodically. The solicitor had promised to resolve the financial issues as swiftly as possible. And Lord Merryweather was but one man; his disapproval did not necessarily reflect majority views in Parliament.

As for Aunt Lavinia's meddling, he would respond directly to her letter expressing his confidence in the match and his intentions to wed Genevieve with or without external approval. Their happiness was not dictated by the closed-minded prejudices of others.

Gradually, the knots in Sebastian's stomach began to loosen. The obstacles, though inconvenient, were ultimately surmountable. Delayed contracts could be renegotiated. Individual dissenters could be persuaded or ignored. With prudence and patience, he and Genevieve would be together at last.

Buoyed by renewed conviction, Sebastian turned toward home. There was much to be done if he was to secure their future. They would prevail, and any who dared try to tear them asunder would only strengthen their resolve further. This latest trial was but a test of that resolve, one he intended to meet and master.

His stride now sure with conviction, Sebastian continued on through the bustling streets of London. The future was theirs for the taking. All that remained was reaching out to grasp it, and never letting go.

The next day, Sebastian sat in his solicitor's office, fingers drumming impatiently on the arm of his chair as Mr. Gibbons reviewed the revised contracts. His mood was already grim after another terse letter from Aunt Lavinia reiterating her disapproval. He was eager to settle this business so he could return his focus to securing his future with Genevieve.

After what seemed an interminable amount of time, Gibbons finally set the documents aside with a satisfied nod. "Everything appears in order, my lord. The properties in question have been set aside in a trust, so they will not affect the marriage settlements."

Sebastian released a breath he hadn't realised he'd been holding. "Thank you, Gibbons. I am most eager to get the contracts formalised."

"Naturally." The solicitor offered an understanding smile as he gathered up the paperwork.

Triumph flashed through Sebastian at this first hurdle being cleared. He stood and shook Gibbons' hand firmly. "Excellent. Your swift handling of this matter is greatly appreciated."

Gibbons inclined his head. "Of course, my lord. I wish you and Lady Genevieve much happiness."

Buoyed by this initial success, Sebastian's mood remained bright as he departed for home. One obstacle down. If he could get Lord Merryweather on side, convince Aunt Lavinia to stop her meddling, and secure Lord St. Claire's approval...He allowed himself a small, satisfied smile. Perhaps he and Genevieve would be wed sooner than anticipated.

Over the next few days, Sebastian wrestled with rising frustration as he made repeated efforts to ally with Lord Merryweather and the other dissenting MPs. Despite his best logical arguments and most persuasive charm, they remained unmoved.

"While I admire your determination, Mordesley, you must see how an alliance with the St. Claire chit looks to the outside world," Lord Aynslie said with a shake of his jowly head. "There have been lots of questions since the boy got back. Lord Ashford duelled someone five years ago, they all ran off to Rome, now they're back and the boy is said to be a demon at business. Best end things now, before your prospects for advancement take a hit."

Sebastian bit back an angry retort. He would not dignify their pompous concerns with the response they sought. "My only aim is to marry the woman I love and who loves me in return. If that hinders my political prospects, so be it."

His peers shared uneasy glances, muttering among themselves. Lord Merryweather gave him a long, considering look. "Your feelings do you credit, Mordesley. Would that more young men valued affection and mutual understanding in matrimony. You could become Prime Minister if you play your cards right. Just make sure whatever scandal the St Claire's ran from does not catch up with you." He sighed. "Very well, I shall stand down my objections if the lady proves worthy of your regard in time."

It was a tepid endorsement at best, but still a minor victory. With patience and care, Sebastian might still turn the political tide in his favour. Buoyed by hope, he continued his campaign of cordial persistence, determined to show there was nothing to fear from his marriage.

Back at home, Sebastian found little solace from his worries. Aunt Lavinia continued bombarding him with letters decrying his "unwise infatuation," demanding he do his duty and marry someone suitable within his own social circle, despite Lady Genevieve being someone suitable in his social circle. When he responded with steadfast refusals, she threatened to come to London herself and intervene.

Sebastian crumpled the latest missive with a snarl. How dare the infernal woman attempt to control his fate through manipulation and hysterics? He began composing a stern response forbidding Lavinia from leaving her estate. He would not permit her to meddle further, family or not. If she could not support his decision, then she would simply have to be excluded altogether.

A knock interrupted his furious scribbling. "This was just delivered for you by private courier, my lord."

Sebastian took the proffered envelope suspiciously. His gut clenched when he recognised Lavinia's handwriting. What new vitriol had she spewed now?

Sebastian,

If you will not listen to reason, perhaps you will reconsider for the lady's sake. Lady Constance recently contacted me with something she had come across. She had thought to keep it secret, however; she is afraid that the artist in question may wish to earn more money by leaking the secret if the lady becomes a marchioness. Please see the enclosed letters.

Faithfully,
    Lavinia

Sebastian unfolded the other sheaf of paper in the envelope. It was a contract engaging Genevieve as a model for a notorious portrait artist- a man known for convincing naïve young women to disrobe under the pretence of "art." Next was a letter penned in Genevieve's hand, vividly detailing a supposed tryst with the artist.

Sebastian's vision went red with fury. This had Lavinia's fingerprints all over it. She must have coerced Constance into helping her concoct this smear campaign, preying on his one vulnerability - protectiveness for Genevieve's reputation.

Clenching the false documents, Sebastian strode for the door. Enough was enough. It was time he had a direct, potentially explosive conversation with his meddling aunt.

"My lord?" His butler hovered anxiously. "Is everything all right?"

"No, it is not." Sebastian snatched up his greatcoat and hat. "But I am going to put a stop to these hysterics once and for all. I've tolerated my aunt's interference long enough."

"Shall I summon your carriage?"

"No need. I'd prefer to handle this alone." Sebastian tucked the papers inside his coat. "If anyone should call, tell them I am unavailable on urgent family business."

The butler's eyes widened slightly but he merely bowed. "Of course, my lord."

Sebastian hastened outside, heading straight for the mews. If he rode hard, he could reach his aunt's estate by nightfall. His blood still boiled over her underhanded ploys to sabotage his engagement. But even Lavinia deserved the chance to explain herself before he took more drastic measures.

The icy wind biting his cheeks helped cool his temper as he rode. He would give her one opportunity to cease interfering in his personal affairs. If she persisted, then he would have no choice but to cut ties, even at the cost of damaging family bonds. His loyalty and devotion were not limitless gifts to be exploited.

By the time Sebastian arrived, weary but composed, dusk had fallen over the countryside. He found Lavinia in her drawing room, affecting an air of fragility. Her eyes widened at his abrupt entrance.

"Sebastian! What on earth—"

"Enough games." He withdrew the false documents and slammed them down before her. "This is your most underhanded ploy yet. Does our family connection truly mean so little to you?"

Lavinia pressed a hand to her chest. "I don't know what you mean. I merely sent you some helpful information about your lady love's past. If you spurn my assistance, I cannot be held responsible for what revelations may surface."

Sebastian leaned down to meet her gaze squarely. "I know precisely what you hoped to achieve with these fabrications. Consider this your one and final warning." He straightened. "Cease these attempts to control my fate, Aunt. I am through humouring your histrionics. I am not sure what advise you can provide given your lack of husband, do not bite the hand that feeds you."

He left without another word, refusing to be drawn into the morass of justifications and excuses she surely yearned to spew. The fresh night air helped clear the remaining haze of anger as he rode for home. He had said his piece with restraint and finality. There would be no further contact between them until Lavinia accepted the futility of her efforts and changed her ways.

By the time Sebastian arrived home in the early hours of the morning, fatigue had replaced his early fury. He wanted nothing more than to lose himself in Genevieve's smile and reminder himself what truly mattered. The obstacles between them were crumbling one by one. Soon, not even meddling relatives could spoil their happiness.

Sebastian penned Genevieve a brief but ardent note, hoping the reminder of his unwavering devotion might lift her spirits as hers did his. No amount of interference would sway him from making her his wife. Their futures were entwined, their fates sealed. And he would permit nothing and no one to tear them asunder.

Lavinia had played her final hand and lost. No more would he allow her histrionics to distract him from securing his future. All his focus would now be trained on the light guiding him steadily home - his darling Genevieve. Nothing else signified but the woman who held his heart.

Come what may, in this life or the next, he would find his way back to her. Always.

Chapter Sixteen

The whispers followed them wherever they went. Sidelong glances and knowing looks were cast their way at every ball or assembly, a susurrus of scandalised gossip in their wake. Genevieve kept her head high, though her cheeks burned with mortification. She had known it would come to this and steeled herself for the judgment of Polite Society. But their censure cut deeper than she had anticipated, the wound made more painful by its unfairness.

For she and Sebastian had done nothing to warrant such condemnation, nothing but follow their hearts in finding love. If that was to be a crime, so be it, but she would not cower under their unjustified scorn.

Sebastian's hand at the small of her back, his quiet strength and assurance, were her only bulwark against the sea of disapproval that threatened to overwhelm. With him beside her, she could face anything. But she worried for him, for the damage to his reputation and standing, all for the sake of her love.

"Do not trouble yourself on my account," he murmured, reading her thoughts with his usual perspicacity. "What do I care for their petty sniping? You are the only thing of value in this world to me, Genevieve. As long as I have you, nothing else signifies."

His words brought solace to her anxious heart, chasing away the last shadows of doubt. The path ahead would not be an easy one, fraught with obstacles and lined by jealous enemies. But together, she and Sebastian would weather any storm.

Lady Constance watched them from across the ballroom, her gaze sharp and predatory. Since the whispers began, she had been hovering at the fringes of their sight, a vulture waiting to feast on their misery. Genevieve stared back, refusing to cower under that malicious scrutiny. She would not give Lady Constance the satisfaction of seeing her discomfort. Beside her, Sebastian tensed, his hand tightening around hers. No doubt he too had noted their observer and the venom in her eyes.

"Pay her no mind," Genevieve said. "She cannot touch us."

A grim smile curved Sebastian's lip. "She will not give up so easily. Constance has always been spiteful, even as a child. Now that she has scented weakness, she will pursue her vengeance to the bitter end."

Genevieve sighed, leaning into his embrace. "Then we shall meet her head on. I will not run from this, Sebastian, not when what we have is worth fighting for."

His eyes softened as they met hers, filled with tenderness and awe. "You are far braver than I, my love."

Lady Constance watched and seethed, her face pinched and sallow with envy. Let her scheme and plot as she would. Genevieve had found her heart's home in Sebastian's arms, and no amount of malice could drive her out. The path ahead would be fraught with obstacles, but their love would sustain them. Of that, she had no doubt.

The whispers began soon after. At first, they were faint as the rustle of silk skirts, easily dismissed. But they grew in frequency and volume, a discordant susurrus that followed Genevieve wherever she went.

According to the rumours, she had seduced Sebastian to secure her fortune, caring nothing for his heart or honour. Some claimed she had used witchcraft or potions to ensnare him, beguiling his senses until he could not tell illusion from truth. Something she had supposedly picked up in Rome. A few went so far as to say she was no better than a lightskirt, granting favours to any gentleman with a full purse and a handsome face.

With each accusation, Genevieve flinched as at the crack of a whip. But she kept her head high, refusing to show weakness before the vipers who sought to tear her down.

Sebastian fumed at the insults aimed against her, demanding satisfaction from those who spread the most vicious lies. But Genevieve stayed his hand, unwilling to see violence bred from malice.

"We knew there would be those who resented our happiness," she told him. "Do not give Constance and her ilk power over you. Our love is not so fragile as to be destroyed by idle gossip."

"You deserve far better than this," Sebastian said, his eyes blazing. "To think they would dare -"

Genevieve placed a finger on his lips, stilling his angry words. "As long as I have your love, nothing else matters. Let Constance whisper to the winds. We have the truth of it, and that is enough."

His expression softened as he gazed at her, wonder and fierce devotion chasing away his ire. "You shame me with your wisdom and strength, my darling. If I could but shield you from all the cruelties of this world…"

She smiled, tracing the line of his jaw. "You have given me your heart - what greater gift could I ask for? That is armour enough against any spite or malice."

Sebastian caught her hand, pressing a kiss to her palm. "Ever my inspiration. With you by my side, even the darkest days seem bright." Despite the rumours and condemnations, Genevieve had found her refuge.

Genevieve returned home that afternoon to find her mother waiting in the drawing room, lips pursed in displeasure. Before Genevieve could utter a greeting, Lady Penelope launched into a tirade.

"Must you persist in this foolish infatuation? You have a duty to your family and station, Genevieve, not to mention your own reputation. The gossip surrounding you and Lord Mordesley is unacceptable. You must put an end to it at once. I permitted it when I thought it would be over with quickly, a trifle, then you would see the error of your ways."

Genevieve weathered the scolding in silence, years of practice lending her patience. When her mother paused to draw breath, she said calmly, "I will not marry a man I do not love, Mama. Not for any reason or duty you cite."

"You unreasonable girl!" Lady Penelope threw up her hands. "Lord Avery was an excellent match. He would give you wealth, status, and security. He may still take you back, his mother is anxious to see him married. You know she and I have been friends since childhood. Love will come in time, as it always does."

"It did not for you," Genevieve said quietly.

Her mother's eyes flashed. "How dare you!" But Genevieve glimpsed the old sorrow there, fleeting yet undeniable. She softened her tone.

"I only mean that you, of all people, must understand how love shapes a life. Why would you wish me to embark on a loveless marriage?"

"Because I want what is best for you," Lady Penelope said. "Because the world is not kind to those who defy convention."

"With Sebastian, I have found more than convention ever could offer." Genevieve clasped her mother's hands. "I beg you, do not ask me to give up my heart's deepest joy. Not for any reason."

Lady Penelope studied her for a long moment, resignation marring her usual composure. She sighed. "Very well. I can see you will not be moved from this course." Her gaze sharpened. "But know that I cannot condone it. And if this entanglement of yours ends in heartbreak, I will not sympathise."

"It will not end so," Genevieve said softly. "Of that, I am quite sure."

Her mother made a disparaging noise, but when she left, it was without further argument. Genevieve smiled, hope glimmering inside her once more. Perhaps love would prevail, after all.

Genevieve breathed deep, savouring the quiet that descended upon the parlour. Her mother's disapproval still stung, yet she could not deny the relief that came with gaining her tacit permission to follow her heart.

Still, doubt lingered. She knew the path she had chosen would not be easy. At every turn, she would face judgment and censure for defying convention.

And there was no guarantee that love would prove stronger than the forces arrayed against them. However, much faith she had in Sebastian's affections, the obstacles they faced were formidable. There would be trials and separations, moments of despair where all seemed lost. The future was obscured, shrouded in shadows of uncertainty.

But when she thought of Sebastian, those shadows receded. In her mind's eye, she saw his smile, felt the warmth of his embrace, heard his voice whispering words of love and devotion. With him, she became part of something greater than herself, a light to guide her way through any darkness.

Genevieve rose and went to the window, gazing out at the sun-drenched gardens below. Somewhere amidst that radiance, a bird trilled out a song of joy.

Let others think and say what they would. She had made her choice, and she did not regret it. Come what may, her heart was full. The path was unclear, but she would walk it with Sebastian at her side. Together, they would face each new challenge and find their way forward into the light.

The next morning, Genevieve awoke to sunlight streaming through her bedchamber windows and birds chirping merrily outside. She stretched with a contented sigh, feeling more at peace than she had in months.

Sebastian was hers, and nothing would come between them again.

A knock on the door interrupted her reverie. "Enter," she called, sitting up and shaking out her chestnut curls.

Georgina peeked in, her eyes dancing with curiosity. "Genevieve, did something happen last night? You look as if you have a secret."

Genevieve smiled. "As perceptive as ever, little sister. Come, I shall tell you." She patted the edge of the bed, and Georgina hurried over to perch beside her.

"Well?" Georgina prompted, squeezing her arm. "Do not keep me in suspense!"

"Mother has given her consent for me to accept Sebastian, or rather she does not condone it, but she will not stop it." Genevieve confessed, unable to contain her joy.

Georgina gasped, her eyes widening. Then she let out an excited squeal and threw her arms around Genevieve. "Oh, how splendid! I knew Mother would come around eventually. She could not deny you true love forever."

"My thoughts precisely," Genevieve said with an impish grin. "Now we must begin planning how to announce the courtship to society. I want it to be memorable."

"Memorable it shall be," Georgina promised. "We shall show them that love triumphs overall."

Genevieve's heart swelled with gratitude for her sister's support. With Georgina by her side, and Sebastian's love guiding her, she felt ready to face any obstacle. She had chosen her own path, and it was leading her to a future more radiant than any she could have imagined. Authenticity and love had won the day, vanquishing the demands of propriety. At long last, she was free to be happy. The two women spent the rest of the day planning and scheming.

The next morning, Genevieve awoke with a lightness in her chest and smile on her lips. For the first time, she felt wholly at peace with herself and the path she had chosen.

She dressed and went downstairs, where she found Sebastian already waiting in the parlour. His face lit up when he saw her, and she noticed the crease between his brows had vanished, replaced by a look of contentment.

"My Lord, I did not think we had an engagement this morning. Though I am pleased to see you."

"You seem in good spirits this morning," he observed, rising to greet her.

"As do you," she replied, extending her hand. He took it and brushed his lips over her knuckles, sending a delicious shiver down her spine.

"I slept well for the first time in weeks," he confessed. "Your letter yesterday saying your mother would not stand between us, has lifted a great weight from my shoulders. Now we need only worry about the gossipmongers, and they have always been beneath my notice."

Genevieve smiled, giving his hand a gentle squeeze. "My love for you is an anchor in the chaos, and it shall never falter."

"Nor shall mine," Sebastian vowed. His eyes gleamed with emotion as he gazed at her. "The path ahead may not always be easy, but you have my hand to guide you each step of the way. I will be by your side through every challenge, my darling, if you would permit me to remain there."

"Always," she breathed.

In that moment, as she stood enveloped in Sebastian's embrace, Genevieve knew true joy. The world might whisper and stare, but she had found her heart's home. Her defiance had led her to peace at last.

The door opened and Gregory walked in. "Mordesley. You know, this is the second time I have caught you in an embrace with my sister in this house. Last time ended in us almost killing each other and our family moving to Rome for five years. Where will this one lead? India?"

"Ashford." Sebastian's spine stiffened slightly. "Gregory, I…" He seemed to stumble his words before catching himself, he sighed. "Gregory, I came here this morning to do what I should have done five years ago but was too young and reckless to do. What I've been too afraid to do since you returned." Sebastian swallowed.

"Genevieve, I have been a cad and a rake. I have known women across the town and there are women that I have led on." He turned to face her. He pulled a long thin box out of his pocket. "Please accept this token as a symbol of my love." Opening the box, a ruby necklace lay nestled inside. It was a delicate and intricate piece, not a gaudy statement piece. "And I hope that you will accept my apologies for my past behaviour. I also hope that you will consent to be my wife."

Genevieve stood speechless. Sebastian had opened his heart to her, and in front of Gregory.

"She says yes." Gregory smiled, laughter escaping his lips. "You and I need a long discussion Mordesley to get past the issues of five years ago." He reached out and shook Sebastian's hand. "She's old enough that she doesn't need permission to marry, but I would still talk to our father and get his permission."

"He has it!" Lord St. Claire's voice floated through the parlour door. "I'll talk to him after you Gregory. He can have breakfast with me in my study." His head popped around the door frame. "Though I would like to be the one who tells her mother. I want to see the look on her face." He disappeared back into the hallway. "Mills, where is Lady Penelope? I have some news she will not want to hear."

Genevieve embraced Sebastian again. "So, you can hear it from me. Yes, I will marry you!" Sebastian grinned and returned the embrace.

Gregory walked over and slapped Sebastian on the back. "Why don't you come into my study, and I will show you my duelling pistols. I had them out in readiness, but I guess I will not be needing them now. "Gregory led Sebastian away suggesting a hunting trip later in the year.

Genevieve collapsed into a nearby chair. Holding a cushion to her face, she let out a squeal of delight, kicking her feet in the air. She leapt up and ran for the stairs. "Georgina!" She ran calling her sister, full of delight.

Epilogue

One Year Later:

Genevieve smiled as she gazed out across the sun-dappled grounds of the Mordesley estate, watching a pair of swallows dart and swoop overhead. It had been nearly a year since she became Marchioness Mordesley, and this sprawling countryside manor now felt as much like home as the London townhouse where she'd grown up.

So much had changed in such a short span of time. She glanced down at the simple gold band on her left hand, spinning it idly on her finger. The public announcement of her betrothal to Sebastian had caused quite the scandal amongst the ton. Her mother had refused to speak to her for a month and Lavinia Mordesley was still barely civil at family gatherings.

But Genevieve regretted none of it. Marrying Sebastian had brought her a happiness beyond anything she could have imagined. The gossipmongers could whisper all they liked - nothing could diminish the joy she'd found with him.

"There you are, my darling." Sebastian's voice interrupted her musings as he entered the morning room. "I've been looking for you everywhere."

Genevieve turned, her heart skipping a beat at the look of affection on his handsome face. "Forgive me, I was just admiring the view of your rose gardens. They're looking especially lovely this morning."

He came up behind her and slid his arms around her waist, pulling her back against him. "Not half as lovely as you," he murmured, nuzzling her ear.

She laughed softly, leaning into his embrace. "Flatterer. Don't think your pretty words will get you out of attending the county assembly with me this evening."

"Drat, you've seen through my nefarious scheme." His tone was mirthful as he brushed his lips over her neck. "Very well, if I must endure the tedious company of our neighbours for an evening, so be it. You'll just have to make it worth my while afterward."

Heat bloomed in Genevieve's cheeks at the suggestive note in his voice, accompanied by a flutter of anticipation low in her belly. Their marriage had awoken a passion within her she'd never dreamed existed. Sebastian was a generous and attentive lover, slowly introducing her to the pleasures a man and woman could share. Her initial uncertainties had faded away, replaced by an almost feverish yearning for his touch.

She turned in the circle of his arms to face him, tracing her fingers along his cravat. "I'm certain I can think of some way to make your sacrifice worthwhile," she purred.

Desire darkened Sebastian's eyes. He made a low noise in his throat before capturing her lips in a searing kiss that left her breathless.

When they finally drew apart, Genevieve gripped his lapels to steady herself, thoroughly seduced by his ardour. "Perhaps we might skip the assembly after all," she whispered.

Sebastian's expression turned serious. "As tempting as those sounds, we really must make an appearance, my love. It is our duty."

Genevieve sighed. "Yes, of course." As marchioness, she had a responsibility to be seen amongst the local gentry and maintain ties. Lavinia Mordesley certainly wouldn't do it. "Very well. But we shan't stay a moment longer than propriety demands before retiring home."

"Your wish is my command." Sebastian smiled and offered his arm. "Shall we take a turn about the gardens to work up an appetite before luncheon?"

Genevieve settled her hand in the crook of his elbow, leaning against him contentedly as they meandered along the gravel pathways. Her heart swelled with love for this man who had defied all convention and expectations to marry her. With him by her side, she could endure a hundred dull assemblies.

After a light afternoon repast, Genevieve and her lady's maid began the lengthy process of preparing her for the evening's assembly. Her pale blue silk gown was freshly pressed, her long chestnut hair arranged becomingly atop her head, curls framing her face. Sapphire drops glittered at her ears and around her neck.

Slipping on long white gloves, Genevieve checked her appearance in the looking glass and permitted herself a small smile of satisfaction. The cosseted young lady who had left for her first London season was gone, replaced by a woman who carried herself with grace and assurance. Marriage suited her, it seemed.

A knock preceded Sebastian poking his head into her chambers. "Ready, my dear?" His appreciative gaze slid over her approvingly. "You look exquisite."

"Thank you." Genevieve accepted his proffered arm. "Did you know, this is the same gown I wore to our engagement ball? I saved it as a country evening dress, I could not bear to part with it."

Sebastian's eyes softened. "I remember it well. I'll never forget how beautiful you looked that night, or how you took my breath away when you agreed to be mine." He lifted her hand to his lips. "You have made me the happiest of men, Genevieve."

"And you I," she said softly. Arm in arm, they made their way downstairs and out to the awaiting carriage that would convey them to the assembly rooms. Genevieve's nerves fluttered pleasantly in anticipation of the evening ahead. Her first public outing as the newly minted Marchioness Mordesley was bound to set tongues wagging, but she would face it as she did everything now - with her husband stalwart and supportive at her side.

The county assembly was a smaller and less lavish affair than the London balls Genevieve was accustomed to. Still, she noted surprise and admiration in the eyes of the local gentlemen and ladies as she entered on Sebastian's arm. As they made the rounds, murmurs of "Quite pretty" and "Well suited" followed in their wake.

"You seem to be making a favourable impression," Sebastian noted during a lull between conversations.

"Either that, or they are simply enthralled witnessing the taming of London's most notorious rake," Genevieve teased gently.

Sebastian winced. "Yes, well, I hope I have proven myself reformed in their eyes." He covered her hand with his own. "With you beside me, I have all that I need to stay on the righteous path."

Genevieve's eyes pricked unexpectedly with tears. "Oh, Sebastian."

Before she could say more, the opening chords of a quadrille sounded. Sebastian's solemn mood vanished as he led her eagerly to join the dancers. Soon they were lost in the rhythms of the dance, gliding together as effortlessly as the first time they had waltzed across a ballroom floor.

When the music ended, they paused to catch their breath, eyes locked. The rest of the room seemed to fall away until it was just the two of them, alone.

"I will never tire of dancing with you," Sebastian said. "Having you in my arms feels like coming home."

"Nor will I," Genevieve vowed. She knew with sudden piercing clarity that so long as they faced each new adventure side-by-side, they could weather any storm and find joy.

The rest of the evening passed swiftly. Genevieve was gratified to receive several invitations to take tea or join the ladies in town for shopping from new acquaintances who seemed genuine in their overtures of friendship. Even the crusty dowagers had to admit she made a charming marchioness.

At long last, Sebastian leaned over and murmured "Shall we?" in her ear. Eagerly, Genevieve bid their hosts farewell and allowed him to guide her out to their waiting carriage.

Settling onto the plush velvet seats, Genevieve slipped her shoes off with a sigh of relief. "I must say that was not as arduous as I anticipated."

"See, associating with country folk is not as dull as I led you to believe." Sebastian's eyes glinted with humour.

"Mmm, the company was pleasing enough," Genevieve allowed. "But now I find myself ready to be home, alone with my husband."

Sebastian's gaze smouldered. "Your wish is my command." He pulled the curtains closed and pulled her into his arms.

Later that night, as Genevieve lay nestled in Sebastian's embrace, she smiled up at the canopy above their bed. She knew deep in her soul that she had made the right choice. With Sebastian by her side, she could brave any storm.

This was forever, of that she was now most certain. No matter where life led them, their love would be their compass and their home.

Genevieve had defied convention and expectation by following her heart and found something far more precious than propriety or duty could offer - a partner who saw her, valued her, and cherished her as she was. She had no need to pretend anymore.

As she drifted off to sleep listening to the steady rhythm of her husband's heartbeat, Genevieve sent up a silent prayer of gratitude. This was her happy ending, but also a beautiful new beginning. The adventure was only just getting started.

About the Author

You can connect with me on:

🌐 https://lisettedavenport.wordpress.com

f https://www.facebook.com/Lisette.Davenport

🔗 https://instagram.com/lisette_davenport_author

www.ingramcontent.com/pod-product-compliance
Lightning Source LLC
Chambersburg PA
CBHW072148130726
47909CB00004BB/1263